D0829533

The
BAMBOO
GARDEN

Susan Austin

SONG TREE BOOKS
Berkeley, California

Song Tree Books
Berkeley, California
www.SongTreeBooks.com

ISBN (print): 978-0-9856279-0-4
ISBN (ePub e-book): 978-0-9856279-1-1

Library of Congress Control Number: 2012909351

Cover design by Felicia Hoshino
Interior design by Jennifer Omner
Map by Suzanne Klein

Berkeley, California ~ 1923

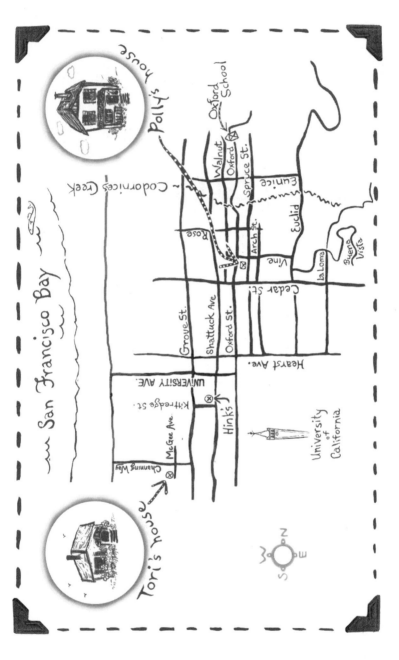

Chapter One

❦ Tori ❦

That morning Tori agreed to Polly's plan for a picnic at the creek, she never suspected everything was about to change. Perhaps the strange hot summer should have been a clue. Still, until the moment she saw the scuffed-up shoe under the berry bush, the summer of 1923 had been nearly perfect for Tori Takahashi.

She usually loved the trolley trip across town to Polly Griffin's house, Mama at her side. Not today. Even though the windows were pushed to the top, no cool air made its way in. Luckily Polly promised they would start a new theatrical production, which meant staying inside her big, cool house choosing costumes. Tori loved that part.

"We do look smashing, don't we?" Polly asked as she straightened the bright yellow headband stretched across her forehead and tied in the back. Tori peered into Polly's bedroom mirror. Two girls stood side-by-side, arms linked, posing in Mrs. Griffin's old dresses. Tori hated looking so tall next to Polly, even though they were both eleven. Still, she liked how the jade green dress with sparkling white beads looked on her. It helped that Mama had cut her black bangs evenly for a change.

Polly patted her new bangs, far too curly to lie flat like Tori's. More brown curls peaked out from under the yellow headband. She had told Tori that when her braids were gone and her hair was bobbed short like everyone else's she would look older. Polly had guessed right. Her new haircut did the trick.

"Yep, we look terrif!" Tori agreed. "But what's the play about?" Carefully, she removed a long white feather she had stuck into her purple headband and replaced it with a shorter blue one.

"Oh, something about a murder at a fancy party." Polly took off her headband and tossed it into a wooden chest. "One of us is going to die. It'll probably be me. I'm pretty good at that." She kicked her mother's high heels into the air one at a time, then let her blue chiffon party dress slip off her shoulders and onto the floor in a heap.

"Say, are you getting hungry?" Polly asked. "I'm starved. How about a picnic? Wait! How about a picnic at the creek? Come on, Tori! We can't let a little hot weather spoil our fun."

Tori imagined the cool water running over her feet. "I guess the creek does sound kind of nice. Wait, hold on! Let's pick some of those blackberries we saw last week. They've got to be ripe by now."

"Don't forget Jerry. He'll want to come, too. But first we've got to drag him away from that wireless radio."

Polly was right. Jerry hadn't stopped talking about the radio for weeks. Tori quickly took off her costume and began to get dressed, but Polly was faster even though she talked the whole time.

"I'll bet Mrs. Hastings left some of her fried chicken in the icebox."

"And maybe some of her snickerdoodles?" Tori did love those cinnamon-covered cookies, and the Griffins' cook made the yummiest. If only her mother would learn how, but how could she when cleaning and sewing for the Griffins kept her so busy?

"I'll start packing the lunch. You look in the pantry for the berry buckets," Polly said as she raced down the back stairs leading to the kitchen. Tori followed, buttoning her dress on the way.

Buckets in hand, Tori got back to the kitchen as Polly latched the icebox shut. "I'm glad Mrs. Hastings isn't here today," she whispered. Tori nodded, remembering the time Mrs. Hastings yelled at Polly for poking around the icebox. "Now Polly, you stay out of there," she had said, hands on her wide hips, face scowling. "That block of ice won't last a day if you keep opening the door!"

Tori watched Polly wrap the last piece of chicken in waxed paper. A sudden pounding on piano keys made Tori jump. Polly didn't even flinch. Instead, she whispered into Tori's ear, "Must be Agnes Wetherby. Poor Mother. We've got to stay out of there for now. Guess we'll just have to tell your mom we're going."

Tori was used to seeing Mama dust or mop. But lately, Mrs. Griffin had her sewing a lot more. They found Mama in the sewing room bent over the machine, her feet busy rocking the treadle up and down. She didn't notice the girls watching from the doorway.

"Tell your mother we're going to the creek."

Polly seemed to like when Tori talked to Mama in Japanese. "Why, you're the only kid I know who speaks two languages," Polly told her once. "Besides, I like hearing your mother talk to you that way. She's different then." Tori had noticed that, too. Mama seemed surer of herself when she talked in Japanese — not as quiet, livelier.

She told Mama about the picnic, who listened then smiled. "*Tanoshinde kudasai. Ki o tsuket,*" she said.

"What'd she say?" Polly asked as the back door slammed behind them. Tori held onto one of the basket handles, Polly the other, berry buckets balanced on top.

"Oh, just that we should have a good time and be careful."

Polly tugged on her handle on the way to Jerry's house, a two-story faded green building directly behind her house. The gate between the two gardens clicked open. Tori looked up to the second-floor apartment where Jerry and his mother lived, curious if he would part with his precious wireless for them.

Arriving at the bottom of his stairs, Polly cupped her hands and shouted, "Hey, Jerry! You up there? Come on out! We're going on a picnic. Maybe pick berries!"

Seconds later Jerry raced down the steps, a cap covering most of his black hair and a berry bucket swinging at his side. Hardly down the last step, he started talking.

"You just can't believe how swell this wireless receiver's going to be! If I bought one at the store it'd cost me a bunch. But I'm making it at home so it'll only be a few bucks. All the fellas in the Boys Radio Club are making one."

Tori rarely saw Jerry that excited. He just jabbered on. "Today I put the copper wire on the chimney. It's the antenna, you know. Won't work without it. Hey, don't tell Mom I was on the roof!"

"Are you going to send messages, too?" Tori asked.

"Sure, when I figure out how. But listen to this. I got earphones for you two, so we can listen together. Isn't that just swell?"

Tori liked hearing Jerry talk about these new crystal sets. Not Polly.

"Yeah, Jerry, just swell. Now hurry up!" Polly kept a brisk pace all the way to the creek.

"Last one in's a slimy snail!" she yelled as she pulled off her shoes and socks, and then dashed into the shallow water.

Jerry followed close behind, then Tori. The water quickly covered her feet and ankles, barely reaching the hem of her dress. The empty bucket banged against her leg as she carefully worked her way over the slippery stones to the other side of the creek. Bright purple berries hung from the bushes along creek's edge, ripe and ready.

"Look here. Big ones! This is where I'm picking," Polly yelled from farther down the creek.

"Boy, these are the best!" Jerry shouted from his spot as berries plinked into his pail.

In a short time Tori's bucket was half full. She bent down to grab some low-hanging fruit. But what was that, under the bush? An old boot? What's a boot doing there? Kneeling to get a closer look, she saw a brown sock above the scuffed boot. Then they both moved, just a little bit. She was sure of it!

In that instant Tori knew a man lay under the bush. Something awful must have happened to him. Maybe he had been unconscious for hours or even days. Did he fall? Was he sick?

Cautiously, she knelt down for a better view, terrified of what she might find but desperate to know. Would it be terrible? Would there be blood? What she saw shocked her more than anything she could imagine. The man who belonged to the boot and sock lay on his back, grinning, plucking berries, and stuffing them into his mouth.

"Mighty sweet berries down here," he mumbled. "Best I ever ate."

Speechless, Tori tried to make her mouth smile at the man. With a shaky voice she called to Polly and Jerry. Then, as a way to warn them, she added, "I've met someone. Come see!"

By the time the man wiggled out from under the prickly bush, Polly and Jerry were there. In one arm, the man tenderly cradled his cap loaded with plump purple berries.

Tori couldn't help staring at his berry-stained lips smiling through a bushy black beard. When he straightened up he was only as tall as Polly.

Something about his broad shoulders, long arms, and overly large hands and feet made him look like a cartoon character from the funny papers. Crudely sewn patches decorated his brown shirt and pants, especially around his knees and elbows. When he crawled from under the berry bush, Tori couldn't help seeing the patches on his backside as well.

That's when she knew. The little man must be a hobo. Lately she'd seen a few around town. Some folks called them *tramps*, but she liked the word *hobo* better. One time Polly wanted to visit the hobo camp by the train tracks. She said it would be fun. Tori didn't think so and neither did Jerry.

There weren't many hoboes in Tori's neighborhood, but she saw plenty where Polly lived. Mrs. Griffin never seemed bothered by them. She fed them all. But not Mrs. Hastings—she shooed them away from the back door. Tori had heard Polly's dad, Professor Griffin, call them "knights of the road." But then she'd also heard plenty of people call them "good-for-nothings."

Just last week she and Polly saw one of them sitting on the Griffins' back porch steps, a cup of coffee in one hand, a sandwich in the other. When those disappeared, he raked the backyard leaves into a big pile. Tori raced upstairs with Polly to the sleeping porch so they could watch him finish the job.

The Bamboo Garden

After dumping the last of the leaves into a wicker basket, he took his time walking to the front of the house. Polly made Tori follow her into Mrs. Griffin's bedroom for a better view. They saw him reach into his pocket and pull out something white. Tori felt sure it was a piece of chalk. Then he left some sort of mark on a tree trunk in front of the house. Standing at that spot a few minutes later, Tori saw that he'd drawn a circle with an x in the middle.

The little man in front of Tori, berry bits on his beard, looked more like the good-for-nothing type of hobo. A glance at Jerry's frowning face told her he agreed. Still, this hobo seemed friendlier than most. After all, he was smiling. Polly smiled back, as if she'd found a long lost friend.

"Want one?" the little man asked, holding out his cap of berries.

"No, thanks," said Jerry.

Tori shook her head no.

"Sure. I'll have one," Polly said as she picked out a berry from his cap.

Relieved that nothing terrible had happened to the man, now all Tori wanted to do was leave. But Polly's red cheeks and silly smile told her that leaving was not something Polly would do easily. Hoboes had always fascinated her, especially since spying on one. Now she talked a lot about them—how great it would be to live like that, hopping on and off box cars, traveling around the country. Would they miss home? Were they ever scared? Did they have lots of pals to travel with? And what exactly was that mulligan stew she heard they liked so much?

"Yep," the man chuckled, "you gotta look for berries where no one else'd think of going. That's the ticket! Think I'll take the rest of these back to my buddies."

"Oh, you mean the hobo jungle? Is that where you live?" Polly asked.

The little man laughed. "Yep. That's what some folks call it. 'Course to us, it's just home. Well, guess I'd better get going."

Removing a tin cup hanging from his belt, he emptied the berries into it. Then he set the stained cap back on his head before crossing to the other side of the creek. Polly trailed after him, Tori and Jerry close behind.

"But what's your name?" Polly asked breathlessly. "I'm Polly. This is Tori, and he's Jerry."

"Good to meet ya, kids," he said, still grinning. "I'm Smilin' Sam."

"Nice to meet you," Polly said. Then, after a brief pause, she added, "Are you hungry Smilin' Sam? Would you like a piece of fried chicken?"

Tori held her breath. What was Polly thinking? How could she ask this man to eat with them? She looked at Jerry. He hadn't said anything, just fiddled with his cap and studied his shoes.

"Why, that's mighty nice of you. After eatin' all those berries, I must confess I'm still hungry. I'd be pleased to have some of that chicken."

Smilin' Sam sat on a nearby boulder, a drumstick in each hand. Tori tried not to stare, but she couldn't help watching him gobble up the chicken as if he hadn't eaten in days. He got talkative after that, telling about the walking stick he'd carved and how his bag with just about all he owns fits onto it, just so. Even though Tori caught a glimpse inside his bag, she couldn't see much.

Polly asked all the questions. She finally got to ask about mulligan stew. He told how he and his buddies would each toss a potato or a carrot into the pot—whatever they found that day. "Never tastes the same," he chuckled.

"So, Smilin' Sam, could you please tell me one more thing?" Polly begged.

"You sure got lots of questions for a little girl."

"Well, I've been wondering. One time, after one of your buddies came to our house, he drew something on a tree in front."

Laughing, Smilin' Sam slapped his thigh. "And you want to know what that was, right? Little gal, that's something you probably shouldn't have seen.

But I suppose it's no big secret. See, we hoboes leave signs here and there that tell the others important stuff about a house. So, what'd he draw?"

"It looked like a circle with an *x* in the middle."

Smilin' Sam snickered, his hand covering his mouth. "Oh, that just means that your house is good for a bite to eat if you're willing to work."

"But then he went next door to the Wetherbys' telephone pole. He drew something like this."

Polly picked up a twig and drew two shapes next to each other in the dirt. One looked like a square with an extra long line at the bottom and, next to it, a triangle.

"Ah, I think I might like to visit that house," Smilin' Sam said, scratching his bearded chin.

"Why? What's it mean?" Jerry asked, the first time he had said anything since Smilin' Sam showed up.

"Well, that square thing now, that's supposed to look like a silk top hat—something a fine gentleman might wear. And that triangle there, that's supposed to be a pile of gold. Guess that's a rich family."

This news made Tori uncomfortable, that hoboes would mark a house like that. Even Polly got quiet. Jerry bumped Polly's arm.

"Time for us to go," he said. "Come on."

"Yeah, I guess so," Polly agreed. Then, flashing a

huge smile she added, "Great meeting you, Smilin' Sam. Maybe we'll see you around."

"Yeah, you might. I'm thinking about staying in Berkeley for a while. This is a mighty nice place. Hot, but mighty nice."

"OK, well, we've really got to go now," said Jerry, firmly pulling on Polly's arm. Tori couldn't put her finger on it, but something about Smilin' Sam bothered her.

"Say, kids, one more thing. Before you go, I wanna give you something. It's just my way of saying thanks for the meal."

With his thumb he flicked a coin right to Polly.

"Ah, you don't need to pay us. It's really OK," Polly protested.

"Nope, that ain't real money. Take a look."

Tori looked at the coin in Polly's palm, the size of a nickel but definitely not a nickel.

"Why, it's wood!" Polly exclaimed.

"Yep, carved it myself."

"Oh, but look! There's a buffalo on one side. Jerry, Tori, look here! Instead of an Indian on the other side, there's a clown head!"

"Right you are! Well, see you around."

Smilin' Sam removed his hat then bowed deeply. He placed his bag on the end of his walking stick, grabbed his cup of berries, and walked downstream along the edge of the creek.

"Just like a true knight-of-the-road," Polly said.

"More like a sneaky scamp, who'll probably follow us home so he can find out where the Wetherbys live," muttered Jerry.

Tori snapped the picnic basket shut. "I wonder what else he keeps in that pack. All I saw were clothes."

Polly laughed. "That's easy—more wooden nickels."

"Must take forever to make," said Jerry. "Let me see it, Polly."

As they walked back to Polly's house, they took turns looking at the nickel. Tori held the coin carefully. A slight breeze could have carried it away.

"Hold up a sec. I've just thought of something," Polly said, stopping suddenly.

The heat had become unbearable. More than anything, Tori wanted to get back to Polly's dark, cool house.

"We've got to take a vow of secrecy."

"About what?" Tori asked.

"About Smilin' Sam and the nickel, of course."

Tori loved it when Polly made everything so mysterious. Despite the heat, she nodded eagerly.

"Sounds OK to me," Jerry said.

The Bamboo Garden

"Let's see, which should it be?" Polly squinted just the way Tori had seen Professor Griffin do when he thought hard about something.

"How about the one when we accidentally broke your mother's vase?" Jerry asked.

"Perfect! OK everyone, hands ready?" Polly stuck out her hand, palm down. Tori rested her hand on Polly's. Jerry's sticky palm sat atop hers.

Solemnly, Polly said the words that always gave Tori goose bumps. "We promise never to tell anyone, under pain of death, or worse . . . " Polly raced through the last part. " . . . that we know Smilin' Sam and that he gave us this nickel. Do you promise?"

"We promise," they all said together.

"Now for the last part," she added. "And we declare this to be our secret now and forever!"

A tingle of excitement crept up Tori's spine.

Chapter Two

❦ Tori ❦

Lying on her back surrounded by bamboo, Tori stared at the circle of blue sky above, then at Polly's face, so close she could count every freckle. Tori loved the bamboo grove tucked away in the corner of Polly's garden. The only way into the circle of bamboo poles was through a hidden passageway in the back. A plaid blanket covered most of the bare ground.

"Come on, Tori," Polly said. "Answer the question. Do you believe in elves?"

Jerry had already told Polly she was loony. Now it was Tori's turn. Hot and sweaty from their game of cowboys and cowgirls, Tori had been enjoying this quiet moment, made all the better with cookies and icy cold lemonade. Mama never made lemonade.

Tori thought over her answer. If she said no, Polly would pester her until she said yes. If she said yes,

Jerry would probably shrug his shoulders and grin. He knew as well as Tori that arguing with Polly didn't get you very far.

"Yes," Tori said, winking at Jerry and hoping Polly didn't see. "I do. But I'm not sure I'd call Smilin' Sam one."

Ever since they'd met Smilin' Sam, Polly tried to convince them he was an elf disguised as a hobo. Nothing was ever simple with Polly. But that's what Tori liked about her, how everything could get so strange and scrambled—like the day she finally got a peek into Polly's "secret" boxes, and all she saw were lots of nuts and bolts and odd pieces of this and that.

"Oh, but he is! And I'm sure I saw him last week, when Donald and his girl, Millie, took me to the top of the Campanile. There wasn't a bit of fog, so the view from the tower was great! I even saw San Francisco."

"I don't think you can see an elf from way up there, Polly," Tori said.

Polly grew quiet. Then, rolling on her back, she said, "I'm just saying that Smilin' Sam looks like an elf. Maybe he isn't a real elf. But it's lots more fun pretending he is. I saw him again at our picnic in Faculty Glade. He hid behind some trees, looking really elfish. No one else saw him. They were too busy listening to Donald play his ukulele."

Jerry licked sugar from each finger. "You know what's so keen about the bamboo grove? How no one can tell we're here. It's like our own private clubhouse."

"Giant bamboo's like that. Papa says you can almost hear it grow," Tori said.

"How does your father know that?" Polly asked.

That's when Tori realized that in the two years they'd been friends, she had never talked about Papa.

"He works in a nursery. He's told me a lot about bamboo. There's all kinds."

Polly counted the cookies on the plate. "Six cookies left. Two for each."

Tori would eat her two slowly, savoring each bit.

For a few minutes, the only sound came from the crunching of cookies. Tori enjoyed the peaceful moment. Why couldn't summer last forever? After tomorrow's church picnic, it would be Monday and the first day of fifth grade.

Polly ended the silence. "I think you're right, Tori. This has to be giant bamboo. I mean, isn't it the tallest bamboo you've ever seen? What's the name of your dad's nursery?"

"The Garden Place. They've got lots of bamboo."

She'd been there a few times, mostly to bring things to Papa, like a message or his lunch. The owner, Mr. Carlson, was friendly and always spoke to her father as if he were important. Tori had pestered poor Papa about planting bamboo in their own garden. He didn't like the idea, worried that the bamboo might spread.

"What's your dad like, Tori?" Polly asked.

"Oh, just like any other dad, I guess. He works a lot." She thought a moment, and then added, "He didn't always work in a nursery. A long time ago, when he lived in Japan, he studied law. But, today he knows a lot about trees and plants."

Law—such an important word to use for Papa with his sandpapery hands and suntanned face. She liked to imagine him as the young Tamaki Takahashi with a head of thick black hair instead of those few wisps of gray. Most of what she learned about his early days came in bits and pieces, a word here, a story there. He would talk about those times in the living room, when her little brothers were tucked into bed. Mama would be mending or ironing, Papa slouched in his favorite chair, feet resting on the small wooden footstool he'd carved.

"Papa," Tori would say. "Tell me about my uncles, about how they got punished for fishing in Ojiisan's koi pond." She liked imagining the three little boys sitting by the pond, dangling their lines in front of Grandfather's fish.

A single question was usually enough to get Papa talking. One story would lead to another, and then another. He would tell Tori about the relatives she'd never met, his family's big house, all their servants, and the beauty of his hometown, Hiroshima. He would also talk about the many long, lonely years in America.

Sometimes when he talked about his family in Japan, Tori thought his eyes looked a little watery. But when he got to the part about arriving in this country, he would sit up a little straighter. He told her about coming to America as a nineteen-year-old, with hopes of making a fortune, of someday returning to Japan rich and happy. For a few minutes he was no longer a tired man of fifty, but young and determined.

"I was one of the early ones," he would say proudly. It hadn't been easy. The only work for him and the other Japanese men meant long days of washing dishes, doing laundry, or cleaning up gentlemen's offices late at night. He had been lonely living in those boarding houses with the other Japanese bachelors, each treasuring their pennies and their dreams.

"But," he would say to her, his furrowed brow now relaxed, "two things happened in my life that changed everything: meeting Mr. Carlson and marrying Mama."

Tori knew this part of the story well. Mr. Carlson had hired Papa to work in his Berkeley nursery. After several years, Mr. Carlson made Papa his manager, a rare opportunity for someone from Japan. But Tori was far more interested in hearing the story about her mother. She'd turn to Mama at this point and ask: "Did you really come to America and marry Papa without knowing him?"

Mama would look impatient and say, "This was not unusual. In Japan, young men and women expected their parents to arrange their marriages. This is what happened for us. It's just that Papa was in Berkeley, California, instead of Hiroshima."

"Weren't you sad about leaving your parents and getting on a ship all by yourself?"

"Yes, but I was excited, too. My family told me Papa was a good man, that he would take care of me. And they were right!"

Tori liked this part of the story most. Papa and Mama would look at each other, remembering . . . Papa no longer lonely, Mama with a new world to discover. One year after their marriage, she was born. They named her *Toriko*, little bird. Her brothers Haruo, Kenji, and baby Yoshi quickly followed. She and the boys were born here, so they were American citizens. "My American children" Papa liked to say with pride. America was their new home. Mama and Papa worked hard, and Tori knew why. "We want you children to have a good life here," they would say.

Finishing the last of her second cookie, Tori didn't share any of those thoughts with her friends. The squawk of a noisy crow overhead, perched on one of the thick green stalks of the bamboo grove, shattered the quiet. The bird's raspy call was quickly followed by another noise — a loud shout and a door slamming from the neighbor's house.

"No, I won't do it. I simply won't do it!"

The sound of feet stomping on wooden steps came next.

"Now what's that about?" Polly asked.

Jerry snickered. "Probably Agnes having another argument with her mother."

Tori had heard Agnes shouting at her parents before, unimaginable in the Takahashi household. Papa might raise his voice, but only now and then and only when absolutely necessary, like when her brothers got a little too lively. Mama would never shout. Mama and Papa expected their children to be obedient and respectful. To do otherwise would be to shame their parents. There could never be a good reason for that!

But Agnes Wetherby was nasty to everyone, including her parents. Sometimes Tori would hide with Polly and Jerry behind the bushes in front of Polly's house. She liked watching Agnes flounce up the porch steps for her weekly piano lesson, which always ended the same way—two angry hands pounding on the keys.

What could have upset Agnes this time? Tori followed Polly and Jerry out of the bamboo grove as quietly as possible. Standing between Polly and Jerry on the bench by the hedge, Tori had a good view of the Wetherby backyard with the most perfect garden she'd ever seen. There were little gravel paths, short hedges, and lots of roses growing in a circle with a birdbath in the middle.

Agnes sulked on her tree swing, dressed in a frilly white skirt and blouse. Yet, even with such beautiful clothes, Tori didn't think Agnes was at all pretty; not with the corners of her mouth pulled down like that, an angry scowl as a permanent guest.

Polly crouched low, signaling them to do the same. Tori made herself as small as possible. She tried to stay quiet but a fit of giggles threatened to spoil everything. Covering her mouth didn't help. Worse yet, the giggles were contagious. Soon Polly and Jerry burst into loud laughter.

"Polly Griffin, are you spying on me? What a rude girl you are!"

Startled, Tori stood up. So did Polly and Jerry. Agnes's angry face stared back at them from the other side of the hedge. Tori had never been so close to the girl.

"Oh, so your playmates are here too, are they? Your *only* playmates I might add." Then, eyeing Jerry she said. "Hi, Jerry. No wait. Maybe I should call you Little Flappy. Those ears of yours could probably flap away flies. Would you like that name, Little Flappy?"

Not waiting for an answer, she said, "Actually, there's nothing little about those gigantic ears of yours."

She laughed at her own joke, then stopped.

Squinting, she stared at Polly and said, "If you keep playing with Flappy, you might grow ears like his! Well, maybe that'd be good. At least you'd be growing something, shorty!"

Then, looking at Tori coldly, she sneered, "You're the maid's little girl, aren't you? I've seen you around. Polly Griffin, you certainly pick the strangest playmates."

The hate behind these words ripped at Tori.

"Can you talk Chinese? Say something in Chinese for me."

The look in Agnes's eyes terrified Tori.

"What, cat got your tongue? That's funny. I hear you jabbering all the time. It's so cute the way you three play together. Jerry, I can't believe you like playing with these little girls. Is that because no one else will play with you? Who'd want to be with a mama's boy anyway? Little oddballs, that's what you are.

From now on, that's exactly what I'll call you—the Three Oddballs."

She stepped off the upside down bucket she had used for seeing over the hedge, and marched back to her house.

Polly was the first off the bench. "Well, that settles it! Something has to be done about Agnes. She's the worst! Oh, I wish she didn't live there. I wish those Wetherbys would go away. Then you could be my neighbor, Tori."

To live next door! Polly had talked about that a lot—an impossible dream, but fun to think about. The dream was full of details like the gate their fathers would build between gardens.

"If you lived here, then the three of us could walk to school every day." From that far away look in Polly's eyes, Tori knew there would be no stopping her. "We'd have such fun. Why, we could . . . "

A high-pitched squeal and a man's deep laugh came from the front of the house.

"Hey, that's Millie and Donald!" Polly exclaimed. "Think they're cooing at each other again? They do love that porch swing." Her eyes twinkled mischievously. "Come on. Let's peek."

The swing's loud squeak muffled their footsteps. A bush loaded with sweet-smelling white blossoms hid them from view.

Tori gladly joined in. Maybe it would stop those awful thoughts swirling in her head — *That Agnes! I hate her! Why did she ask me to speak Chinese? White people think Chinese and Japanese are the same. They even act surprised when I speak English. Sometimes they ask me how long I've been in this country. Papa and Mama's English isn't too good, but they weren't born here. I was!*

Peeking through the bushes, Tori had a clear view of the two sweethearts, both dressed in summer whites. Donald was strumming his ukulele. His song described Millie perfectly; something about being five foot two, eyes of blue, turned-up nose and turned down hose. Millie's head rested on Donald's shoulder while he strummed.

Tori clapped a hand over her mouth, another giggle on its way. How silly Donald and Millie looked! Jerry and Polly glared at her, and then both did the same; hands placed over their mouths to muffle their laughter. Donald stopped playing.

"OK, you little sneaks! You're going to get it!"

He leaped over the porch railing and chased after them. Squealing with laughter, Tori ran with Polly and Jerry along the side of the house. The two were out ahead, kicking up a cloud of dust from the dirt-packed driveway. A flicker of the curtain from behind a large picture window in the Wetherby house caught

Tori's eye. Agnes Wetherby stood by the window, watching everything. Tori tried to look away, but she couldn't. What Agnes did next hurt more than any of her mean words. Hands raised to her face, fingertips at the corner of each eye, Agnes waited. Just as Tori raced by, the girl pulled back her fingers—just far enough to turn her eyes into narrow slits.

Chapter Three

❦ Tori ❦

Tori always liked the streetcar ride back to the other side of Berkeley, mostly because she had Mama all to herself. Mama never said much, tired from a day's work. But she never interrupted and she always smiled in the right places.

Today Tori didn't feel much like talking. She wanted to think, mainly about that scene with Agnes. Ever since her first visit to the Griffin home two years ago, Tori had always felt welcomed. But now Agnes changed all that. As the wheels of the streetcar beat against the metal tracks, Tori rested her head on Mama's shoulder.

She could never forget that first time at Polly's house. It started with a surprising invitation soon after Mama started working at the Griffins'. . . .

"Are you sure you understood Mrs. Griffin correctly?" Papa asked after Mama explained everything. Mama's poor English had gotten her into trouble before. But she'd been studying hard. Even the women at church had begun to ask Mama for help with words they didn't understand.

"Yes, I am sure. Mrs. Griffin made it very clear."

"Doesn't this girl have her own friends?"

"One friend—a little boy who lives behind them."

"Can Mrs. Nishima take care of the boys without Toriko?"

"Mrs. Nishima said she can."

Tori watched Papa empty his bowl of sukiyaki, thin slices of vegetables, and beef sitting in a steaming broth. She glanced at her brothers Haruo and Kenji, eating too fast as usual. Little Yoshi dropped his chopsticks from his high chair again and again. Tori picked them up again and again, waiting for Papa's answer.

Finally, after Tori and Mama had cleared the plates from the table, Papa spoke. "I suppose this would be good for you, Toriko. Your mother thinks Professor and Mrs. Griffin are nice people. Would you like to go?"

Tori fiddled with the chopsticks. Could she tell Papa how she really felt, how she never wanted to meet this girl Polly?

"Yes, Papa, I think so."

"Fine," he said, thumping his hands on the table as he stood up. "Then you shall go to the Griffins' on Saturday."

Her brothers were still fast asleep that morning when Mama unlatched the front door. Cool bay fog had settled around the small wood frame houses that lined the street, almost hiding them from view. The little orange streetcar flew too quickly through downtown Berkeley. Tori hardly had time to look at the shop windows.

When the streetcar made its turn into the Griffins' neighborhood, Tori watched as they passed by one beautiful home after another. After a few blocks, the streetcar jerked to a stop. Tori followed Mama down the wooden steps and onto the dirt road. Mama's warm, dry hand grasped hers as they walked under a canopy of trees. The beauty of Spruce Street had been a big surprise. Her own neighborhood was so different—small homes huddled together and separated by narrow patches of grass or fences, hardly any trees, few automobiles, and fewer garages. And from what she could tell on this short walk, there were no Japanese faces here, not one.

"Come on, Toriko, no dawdling. I don't want to be late."

The Griffin house looked like all the others on Spruce Street—a two-story, wood-shingled place with a deep-set porch. But Tori could tell a child lived there from the red wagon on the front lawn. It was filled with a strange assortment of things like a squished cowboy hat, long piece of rope, hammer, and wood tennis racquet missing most of its strings.

No sooner had Mama showed Tori how to hang her coat on the laundry room hooks, than Mrs. Griffin appeared. "I'm so glad to meet you, dear. I know it's early for a Saturday. But now, you and Polly have lots more time to get to know each other, don't you?"

Tori studied the floor's gleaming black-and-white tiles. What she really wanted to do was take a second look at this lady—her bright blue eyes, short golden curls, and friendly face. She couldn't have been much taller than her own little mother, but so different!

"Hey, Polls, they're here!" Mrs. Griffin shouted up the back staircase.

Tori stood in the Griffins' kitchen, holding Mama's hand.

Even before she saw her, Tori heard the sounds of Polly Griffin: a great thumping of feet on the floorboards overhead, then the clattering of shoes down the wooden staircase into the kitchen. Brown braids flying, cheeks flushed red, Polly jumped off the bottom step and into Tori's life.

Mama had told her they were the same age, but Tori wasn't sure. The top of Polly's head barely reached

Tori's shoulders. The braids caught her attention—a bright red ribbon on one and yellow on the other. Even more interesting were Polly's eyes—as green as the jade ring Mama wore. But the biggest surprise was the chocolate-brown bunny Polly clutched in her arms.

"Oh, Tori, you're here at last! I've been waiting for you all morning! Do you like to swing? I have a keen swing. Next time bring your skates. I wear my skate key around my neck. See, it's on this ribbon. That way I never lose it."

Tori didn't know what to make of this girl, leaving so many questions hanging in the air. Silently, she squeezed her mother's hand.

"Come on, I'll show you around," Polly said, shifting the wiggling bunny onto her shoulder like a baby.

Reluctantly, Tori let go of Mama's hand. She wouldn't embarrass her.

The rest of the morning had been a blur. Books were a big part of that memory; big towers of books in every room. There were books sitting on overloaded shelves, next to chairs, even on the floor. But mostly Tori remembered there were surprises all around. Polly's bedroom had been the biggest surprise of all. It wasn't the bed, so high that she had to use the little wooden step stool to get to the top. It wasn't the canopy of white lace above the bed, sheer enough to see through to the painted yellow stars on the dark blue ceiling. It wasn't even Polly's brown bunny, Fudge, who sat so quietly on the fluffy bed pillows while Tori petted her soft, warm ears. No, what surprised Tori most were the shelves of toys stretching from one end of the room to the other. There were dolls, piles of games, a bat and ball, an Indian headdress with feathers and brightly colored beads, and rows of boxes each neatly labeled "Top Secret." There hadn't been time to peek inside them, because Polly had wanted Tori to see her "real" bed, the one on the little screened-in sleeping porch.

Cool morning air rushed at Tori's face as she followed Polly onto the porch. Canvas shades on rollers hung near the ceiling. Against one of the walls stood a simple iron bed, a multicolored patchwork quilt spread on top.

"Mother and Father think the fresh air's good for me," Polly confided. "I like it here, most of the time. Do you have a sleeping porch in your house?"

From the moment she had entered the Griffin household until now, Tori hadn't spoken a word. For an instant she wondered which language would come out of her mouth when she finally did speak—Japanese or English?

"No," she said softly. "My brothers and I sleep in one of our bedrooms. Mama, Papa, and the baby sleep in the other."

"You have brothers? Oh gosh, you're lucky. I don't have any brothers or sisters. Well, I have Donald, but he's not my brother. He's my cousin. He's living with us 'til he finishes up the university."

Polly sat up, smiled at Tori, and whispered, "Hey, let's go look in Donald's room. He won't mind. I think I'll take my marble bag with me."

She rolled off the bed, dropped to her belly, and scooted underneath. "It's got to be here somewhere. At least, I think so."

By now most of Polly had vanished. Only the soles of her scuffed-up Mary Janes were visible, once shiny black. Tori looked around the sleeping porch and back into the cheery bedroom with its starry blue ceiling. Two places to sleep! Her little bedroom on Channing Way had barely enough room for two beds; hers and the one Haruo and Kenji shared.

Bam! The walls of the sleeping porch shuddered. She held onto the metal frame of the bed Polly had just scrambled under. Had someone thrown a trash can at the house? She watched Polly scoot out from under the bed; bits of dust stuck to her red plaid dress, a leather pouch for marbles clasped in one hand, a long silky ostrich feather in the other. Polly didn't seem the least bit surprised by the racket.

"That's Jerry! Come on! You've got to see the bucket phone."

The Bamboo Garden

Tori followed Polly to a small outdoor balcony off the sleeping porch. On tiptoes Polly leaned over the wood railing.

"I've got it!" she shouted, waving a small piece of white paper.

Tori leaned over the balcony to see where it had come from. Swinging against the side of the house was a battered metal bucket hanging from a rope. The rope circled a metal pulley nailed to the house. It looked just like the backyard clothesline Papa had attached to her house, only this one was much higher and longer. The line stretched across the Griffin garden and fence, over to a faded green two-story building.

"Hey, Tori. Listen to this."

Polly read the note.

> Hi,
>
> What are you doing? Guess what? I fond a brokin spy glass in a box. I am fixing it. I know what I want to do with it. Can you gess?
>
> Jerry

Polly looked up and waved to a boy at the other end of the rope. He waved back from a landing at the top of an outside stairway.

"That's Jerry Berman. He and his mother live

up there, in that apartment with the big porch all screened in. His daddy died when Jerry was just a baby. We've been friends since we were three. Let's write back."

Polly rushed to her desk on the sleeping porch. Using a different color crayon for each letter, she licked each tip before writing. Tori read the words to herself as Polly wrote.

A spyglass! Do you want to spy on someone?
I do!
Come meet my new friend Toree.
Polly

Tori didn't say anything about Polly's spelling. But she couldn't help wondering about Polly calling her a friend. They'd only just met!

"You send it back, Tori. Just pull this here."

As Tori pulled the top rope, the bucket swung on the bottom rope, steadily inching toward Jerry.

Tori knew her brothers were going to love the story about the bucket phone. They were keen on new inventions. Slowly the bucket made its way across the two backyards until finally it banged on Jerry's wall. Tori watched him read the note. He looked up, waved, and disappeared into his apartment.

On that first day Polly had also told her about

Agnes. "Agnes Wetherby thinks she's so great. No one at school likes her. You won't either. She's got to be the meanest girl I know. Jerry's spyglass will be great for seeing what she's up to."

Tori looked at the Wetherby house. Everything about it seemed so grand. Lacey white curtains hid behind squeaky clean windows. In the driveway sat a shiny black automobile, much bigger and fancier than the banged-up one on the Griffins' side.

Everything Polly had said about Agnes on that first day turned out to be true. She was mean and nasty. Until now Agnes had ignored them. Following Mama off the streetcar, Tori now wondered if there'd be more trouble ahead.

Chapter Four

ༀ Polly ༀ

Polly watches Jerry throw open the gate that separates their gardens. He looks nice in his crisp white shirt and still-damp hair carefully parted down the middle. "Hey," he shouts as the gate bangs shut behind him, "let's get going. If we don't hurry, we're gonna be late. Come on!"

He is already running down her driveway to the street as Polly hurries to catch up.

As soon as she arrives, he starts talking. "I just can't wait to see how he hangs from the hands of that clock. I mean, what if he fell from that skyscraper?"

They are on their way to the moving picture show, but not just any moving picture. This one stars Polly's favorite actor, Harold Lloyd. Everyone is going. Well, almost everyone. Polly had begged Tori to join them. But she came up with a million excuses. Mother and

Father went last week. Afterward, Father told Polly the story, about how a young man called "The Boy" does lots of dangerous things for "The Girl," all for love.

Plenty of Polly's school friends are also going to the matinee so there'll be a long line. Jerry hates that! If only he'd slow down. One block of running and already Polly is hot and sticky.

Maybe it wasn't such a smart idea to save their streetcar nickel for the candy counter. With no allowance left, she had to do extra chores to earn money for the show. Mostly she washed and dried dishes for Mother and Mrs. Hastings. Jerry delivered extra newspapers.

"Hey, Jerry, do you think this'll be the week I win?" Polly asks, trying to catch her breath.

She always hopes to be the lucky child, the one whose ticket stub is picked out of the glass bowl at intermission. One time Jerry got the prize—a baseball. Today could be lucky for her. One of those coupons for a free strawberry cone from Edy's Ice Cream Parlor would be terrif!

After a few more blocks, Jerry slows down. Polly is glad. Everything around her seems to be shriveling up from the heat. Flowers droop. Grass is brown and crisp. The streets are strangely quiet. Most people are sitting in the shade of their front porches. "A real scorcher," is what Father said at breakfast, "and more on the way."

Just as they reach another tree-shaded street, Polly spots Professor Cole walking toward them, his white suit crumpled. In one hand he clutches a wilted handkerchief. In the other, he holds a straw hat to fan his damp and cherry-red face.

"Look who's coming!" Polly whispers to Jerry. "That's the new professor, the one I told you about in the bucket phone," and then in a louder voice, "Hi there, Professor Cole."

Even though she'd only met him the night before, he feels like an old friend.

"Well if it isn't Miss Griffin. My but it's good to see a familiar face."

Professor Cole's friendly greeting makes Polly like him even more. Father had invited him to dinner last night. Mother served the meal outside because of the heat. Platters overflowed with end-of-the-summer corn, buttery biscuits, and sliced meatloaf—lots of food for lots of people. Donald and Millie were there, too.

Polly liked Professor Cole right off, and not just because he was younger than most of the professors she'd met. His beard was neatly trimmed, without any gray hairs popping out like Father's. The crinkles around his eyes deepened when he smiled, which was often.

Last night's dinner conversation was so lively, she couldn't get a word in. As she finished off her third piece of corn, Donald grabbed center stage.

"Did you hear what happened today?" Not waiting for a reply, he eagerly went on. "A few hoboes came to town. They made quite a ruckus."

"Hoboes in Berkeley? Fascinating! Why, I'm quite intrigued with hoboes," Professor Cole said. His dark eyes fixed on Donald. Polly wondered if hoboes had anything to do with myths and tales. That's what Papa told her Professor Cole liked most.

"Well, Professor," Donald continued importantly, "we've got plenty of them around. Seems they got rowdy. Folks say this has been happening more and more."

"Maybe our summer weather's attracting them," Millie added, fanning herself with a napkin.

"Generally they're no problem," Father said. "They pretty much keep to themselves."

"Mostly, that's so, Bernard," Mother agreed. "But they do come through the neighborhood now and then. They only want some work and something to eat."

Here was Polly's moment—the perfect place to tell them about Smilin' Sam. She'd been hoping to run into him again. Maybe he'd ask her to visit the hobo camp and maybe even try some of that stew she'd heard about. But the vow! No, she couldn't tell them! Instead, she gnawed on the corn cob. Smilin' Sam and the nickel would be her little secret.

Now, she had Professor Cole all to herself.

"It's good to see you, too, sir," Polly replies. Then, using her best manners she adds, "This is my friend Jerry Berman. Jerry Berman, this is Professor Cole. We're going to the picture show."

"Goodness, I'd much rather be doing that." He fans his hat faster.

"What are you doing?"

"Humph! Apartment hunting!" he says then wipes his neck with the handkerchief. "I've walked everywhere, but I'll tell you, Polly, I'm not having any luck at all. I need something quiet and spacious. Most of what I've seen is fine for students, but not for me. I've just about given up the idea of finding anything in this neighborhood."

"Did ya' see the flat in my building, sir? The one on Oxford?" Jerry asks.

"Well, young man. I don't know about that one. What's it like?"

"We live upstairs, but the downstairs is empty. And the owner never rents to students."

"Now you've piqued my interest."

While Jerry gives the address and directions, Polly fiddles with the wooden nickel she keeps deep in the corner of her dress pocket. She pulls it out.

"Hey, Polly. Whatcha got there?" Professor Cole asks. A second ago he looked as if he would melt onto the sidewalk. But now his face brightens.

"Oh, it's nothing," she says as innocently as possible. Finally—a chance to talk about Smilin' Sam. But a promise is a promise.

"Looks like a hobo nickel. Can I take a look?" Professor Cole extends his hand.

"Sure."

"Where'd you get it?"

Polly looks at Jerry. Frowning, he studies his shoes. Professor Cole turns the nickel over and over. Jerry taps his shoe on the dirt-packed road. Finally she holds out her hand.

"Guess we have to scoot, sir. We don't want to be late."

"Oh, why yes, of course, Polly. Sorry. It's just that this is a special little coin you have here. You do know that, don't you?"

"What do you mean, *special?*"

"Whoever made this carves quite well. See how real that buffalo looks? Now look here, when I turn it over. No Indian head, right? There's a clown head! Pretty funny. Not an easy job on this small surface.

It shows great skill. By the way, you do know this nickel could be magic, don't you?" Professor Cole hands back the coin.

"Magic?" Polly says, all thoughts of the movie gone. She takes another look at the wooden disc.

"Possibly. Of course that only happens if you did something nice for the person who gave you the coin. Did you?"

"We sure did! We shared some of our . . . oof!" Jerry bumps her with his foot.

Professor Cole doesn't seem to notice. "It's said that some hoboes know the trick of putting a charm on these nickels."

"A good charm or a bad one?" Polly studies Professor Cole's face to make sure he isn't joking.

"Generally speaking, a good one, but the charm works only if the person who accepts the nickel in exchange for food or a night's shelter doesn't know it's magical when it's given."

"Wow, a magical charm. What kind of magic does it do?"

"Oh, simple things like bringing luck or good fortune, or maybe something about friendship."

He hesitates before going on.

"These charms do have their peculiarities, though. I've heard some wild stories. It's said that if you don't make the right kind of wish or you hold onto it too long, you could be in big trouble. Why, I heard about one gentleman who ended up penniless after getting one of these. Seems he wished for buckets of money. But when he gave his nickel away to someone who did something nice for him, his luck changed for the better. Strange, don't you think? But interesting, very interesting. I'd like to meet the fellow who made this. Well, I'm off to see that apartment, Jerry. Wish me luck. I sure could use some today."

He tips his hat and continues on his way.

Polly wanted to hear more about what the professor meant by the right kind of wish, but Jerry is pulling her arm. As she tucks the wooden nickel back into her dress pocket, she's sure it feels a little heavier.

Chapter Five

⚘ Polly ⚘

Thoughts of the coin vanish as Polly scrambles to keep up with Jerry. A streetcar rumbles by, kicking up road dust. Polly is glad there aren't too many cars out today or the dust would be even worse.

One more block and they'll be on Shattuck Avenue with all its shop windows. Now Polly picks up the pace. The jeweler's shop comes first. She glances at the clocks lined up in the window. Only twelve-thirty and they are near Hinks Department Store.

"See that," she says, grabbing Jerry's shoulders and pointing him toward the window. "We've got oodles of time. Let's go say hi to your mom before we go to the picture show. Besides, we can cool off in there. They've got those gigantic fans."

Mrs. Berman sells gloves at the department store.

Polly adores her, especially how she makes Polly feel grown-up and important.

"Gloves are a lady's best friend," Mrs. Berman had told Polly more than once. Polly knows that women wouldn't be seen downtown without them. Lots of times Polly watched Mrs. Berman cutting glove patterns on her kitchen table. Mother explained to Polly that Mrs. Berman does this work to earn extra money, selling her handmade gloves to Berkeley's wealthiest women.

"Come on, Jerry. Let's go see your mom," Polly says again, amused to see Jerry staring at the department store window in front of them. The manikins, dressed in back-to-school clothes for boys, are posed with baseball bats and caps.

"OK, but first let's go up to the mezzanine floor," Jerry says, following her into the spacious store.

Polly likes it up there, too, especially when she leans over the balcony's brass rail to watch the busy main floor below—the scurrying salespeople, the shiny glass countertops, the bright colors of clothes piled high on the shelves and tables.

Jerry's mother stands behind the glove counter in the far corner of the store. Raising her hand to wave, Polly hesitates when she notices Mrs. Berman is busy with customers. Polly follows Jerry down the stairs, polishing the smooth brass rail with her hand.

Usually, whenever Jerry and Polly stop by the glove counter, Mrs. Berman greets them with a big smile, one a lot like Jerry's. Today is different. Mrs. Berman doesn't even see them.

Standing at the counter are a woman and a young girl inspecting several pairs of gloves laid out on the glass top. Jerry touches Polly's arm and points to a large potted palm tree nearby. She follows him behind the palm. From here Polly sees most of the glove counter, but she pushes a palm leaf away from her face for a better view.

The woman is tall, made taller by a fluffy purple feather sticking from her hat. The shiny black eyes of a fox fur wrapped around her coat collar stare back at Polly. She can't imagine why anyone would wear a fur on the hottest day of the year. What a show-off!

Still, Mother would think the girl looked smart in her matching blue and white hat and dress. Even her hair is bobbed to the perfect length, just below her ears. Probably a mother and daughter. They seem familiar, but why does Mrs. Berman look so unhappy?

When the girl stamps her foot, Polly understands everything. The customers are Agnes Wetherby and her mother.

"Jerry, look who it is!" she whispers into his ear.

"I can see," he whispers back.

Heaps of gloves are scattered all over the counter-top, and most of the long, narrow glove drawers behind Mrs. Berman are pulled out. From behind the palm, Polly can hear every word.

"Well, I thought Hinks would have a much better selection than this for my little Agnes," says Mrs. Wetherby. "You just don't seem to have her size. I really didn't want to go to San Francisco. But really, the choice of gloves at the City of Paris Department Store is far superior to these poor things."

"But Mother, I really want gloves today! You promised!"

Mrs. Berman's voice is quieter, but Polly makes it out.

"Agnes, dear, these gloves look quite nice on you. I know they're a size larger than you are used to buying, but you have grown, and they do flatter your long, thin fingers."

Agnes scowls. "Well, I don't like them, and they're *not* my size. Mother, let's go!"

Without a thank-you the two turn and walk away from the piles of gloves. Mrs. Berman glances nervously at a waiting customer drumming her fingernails on the glass.

Jerry's mouth is set in a straight line, his fists clenched at his sides.

"Come on," he says in a hoarse whisper. "She looks busy."

Without another word he turns around and heads to the front doors. Polly follows into the bright, hot day. She knows he's boiling mad but has no idea how to make things better. Helplessly, she decides to pretend nothing happened.

Before now she never thought Mrs. Berman might have to deal with rude and nasty people at Hinks. Had Jerry? Everyone knows how cruel Agnes can be, like when she called him "Flappy" or when she said those mean things to Tori. But for some reason, Polly didn't think grownups could be as mean as kids. Mrs. Wetherby just showed they can.

By the time they buy their tickets, find seats with friends in the front row, and listen to the organ player warm up his fingers on the big keyboard, Polly feels better. How wonderful to leave the real world outside and escape for a few minutes into the crazy world of the moving pictures. The box of chewy chocolate babies she picked out at the refreshment stand helps.

Then Polly gets her next surprise of the day. Harold Lloyd's daredevil tricks as The Boy are scarier than she imagined—especially the stunts high above a busy street. Every silly thing The Boy does makes her believe he will plummet to his death, and all in the name of love. Polly has trouble covering her eyes and reading what the actors are saying at the same time.

She enjoys a good laugh when the mouse climbs up The Boy's pant leg. But she can't help screaming with the audience when The Boy looks as if he's about to fall. When the clock scene finally arrives, she looks at Jerry instead of at the screen, his face lit by the black-and-white images flickering before him. He isn't thinking about that nasty scene at the glove counter anymore. He is lost in Harold Lloyd's crazy, upside-down world where The Boy is holding onto a hand of the skyscraper's gigantic clock. No wonder they call the picture *Safety Last*.

At this very moment, he turns her way. Surprisingly, he puts his hand on top of hers. Sweaty and sticky, it stays there. Polly is confused. Is her heart banging around like this because of Harold Lloyd's scary antics or Jerry's hand?

Chapter Six

❦ Tori ❦

"Come on, Polly. Tell me all about it," Tori begged. "Were you scared? Did The Boy make The Girl fall in love with him?"

The hammock had been Tori's idea. What better way to keep Polly in one place? Cooling shade from a giant oak tree, the sweet scent of orange blossoms, and the big, colorful hammock—the perfect way to hear Polly's story. Tori wanted to hear every little detail.

Someday Tori would see a moving picture show. "You have far more important things to do with your pennies, Toriko," Papa had said each time she begged to go. Luckily, on Sunday Mama had to finish making a dress for Mrs. Griffin. So after church she and Mama rode the streetcar to Spruce Street.

Fudge was in the garden with them, another of

The Bamboo Garden

Tori's ideas. The bunny hadn't been eating, so Tori thought a romp outside might help. Polly didn't seem too worried. "Rabbits don't like this heat," she had told Tori. "What if you had to wear a fur coat on a day like this?" That made sense; still, Tori thought a nibble of green clover would do the bunny good. She watched to make sure Fudge found the greenest, juiciest clover patch before climbing into the hammock.

"Oh, I'll tell you everything, I promise," Polly said. Then, using a voice that always gave Tori the shivers, Polly added, "But first, look at this." Slowly and dramatically she pulled the wooden nickel from her pocket.

"Oh Polly, put that silly thing away. Come on now. Tell me about the picture show!"

Tori didn't usually mind Polly's teasing, but today was different. She hadn't come all the way across town to hear more about that hobo. Anyhow, she'd made up her mind about him at the creek. He wasn't to be trusted. Anyone who smiled all the time, even when he wasn't saying something funny, had to be a suspicious character. Besides, why did he get so interested in the Wetherbys' house after hearing about the drawing of the silk hat and pile of gold?

Playfully, she reached for the coin. As Polly snatched her hand away, the wobbly hammock dumped them both onto the parched lawn below. She laughed until her sides ached.

"OK, Tori," Polly said with a big sigh after the girls had climbed back into the hammock. "First the picture show, and then the nickel."

Deciding it was her turn to tease Polly, Tori asked, "What was the scariest part? Did you close your eyes?" Polly rarely admitted being scared.

"Of course not! Well, I might have peeked through my fingers now and then because you can't imagine how the world looked from way up on that skyscraper. My favorite part was when the mouse climbed into The Boy's pant leg."

Tori closed her eyes, imagining how everything looked on the big screen.

"How do you think they got the pigeons to land on The Boy's head?"

"Peanuts! Someone had tossed these peanuts onto him, and the pigeons came to eat. It was hilarious."

Tori tugged on the rope tied to a nearby tree—another Polly Griffin invention. The hammock rocked gently.

"By the way, I know why it's called *Safety Last*. Believe me, being safe was the last thing The Boy thought about!"

Tori concentrated on remembering every detail, not only for herself but for Haruo and Kenji, too. She knew they'd never stop pestering her if she didn't tell them all about the picture show.

"I wasn't scared," Polly boasted as she put the finishing touches on her story. "Everyone knows it's just pretend. They weren't going to let him fall. That would be terrible. Harold Lloyd's a big Hollywood star!"

"Did Jerry like it?"

"Oh yeah, he loved it." Then Polly did a very un-Polly thing—she clammed up. Impatient, Tori yanked the hammock rope hard.

"Come on! You can't stop now!"

"Sorry. Hmmm, let's see. Jerry, well, he couldn't stop talking about the stunts the whole way home. We got back just in time to see Professor Cole again. I think he might be moving into Jerry's building as soon as he . . . "

"Who's Professor Cole?" Tori interrupted.

"Ah, yes, the mysterious Professor Cole and the wooden nickel." Polly held the coin so they could both see. "It's magic, Tori! It really is! Professor Cole said so."

"So who is this Professor Cole?" Tori asked again, knowing how Polly liked to make things puzzling. Simple things always became strange and thrilling with Polly.

After Polly told the story about the new professor,

his apartment hunt, and what he had said about hobo charms, they stared at the coin. Tori broke the silence.

"You didn't break our vow, did you?"

"Why, Tori!"

"Sorry. So, how's it work?" and then, "What's a bad wish?"

Although Tori didn't actually believe in magic and wishes, she knew Polly did. Polly made wishes all the time, like blowing out candles on her birthday cake or just before her very first taste of a summer fruit like cherries or apricots. She'd shut her eyes tightly, clenching her fists as she wished. "A non-believer" is what Polly had called Tori more than once, usually when Tori laughed at Polly for making another wish. Even so, Tori wanted to believe in the professor's tale. But then there was the part about making the wrong kind of wish.

"I'm not sure what it means, but I've decided not to worry about that. Anyhow, I already know what I'll wish for. Can you guess?" Polly asked. "I'll bet you can!"

"Oh, Polly, not that same wish again. That'll never happen," Tori said, shaking her head. Now she knew how Mama must feel when her brothers said something especially silly. Silently she wondered if Polly's wish might be the bad kind Professor Cole had described.

"Yep, that's the one! I'll never, ever stop wishing you lived in the house next to mine. I want those Wetherbys to just disappear, like smoke!" Polly snapped her fingers. "*Poof!* They're gone! And then you and your family can move in. We can be neighbors. We can play together whenever we want. Don't you think that has to be the best wish in the whole world?"

"But Polly," Tori protested, "that's too big a wish. Why don't you start with something small, like a new bicycle?"

"I'll tell you what. I'll hold onto the nickel for another week and keep wishing my wish. I don't think that's too long. If it doesn't come true, then you or Jerry can have a turn. It's just got to work for one of us! Hobo magic is powerful, I'll bet."

For the rest of the afternoon they searched the garden, choosing the best greens for Fudge who showed little interest in the clover. That worried Tori. Poor hot bunny.

Tori was glad Polly didn't ask what she'd wish for when it was her turn. She hadn't decided yet. Besides, what if she made the wrong kind of wish? While she and Polly worked on building fairy houses from twigs and leaves, Tori thought about wishes. What if she could really have a wish, just one wish? Would it be for herself? Maybe. For Mama and Papa? Maybe. For her brothers? No, never for them! Why, just this morning Haruo and Kenji had sprayed her with the hose when they were supposed to be watering the lawn. No wishes for those brats. She had time to decide. Even though she really didn't believe in wishes, she trembled at the possibility that Smilin' Sam's wooden nickel might really have the power to make wishes come true.

Chapter Seven

✵ Polly ✵

Mother shouts into the telephone.

"Of course, Mrs. Hastings. I just thought you were late. I'm so sorry. I do hope you'll feel better soon."

The alarm in Mother's voice yanks Polly from the Sherwood Forest with Robin Hood and his merry men. Leaving her book on the couch, she finds Mother in the hallway, the telephone's trumpet-shaped hearing piece pressed tightly to her ear. Her other hand squeezes the slim neck of the telephone's base. Polly tries not to laugh but can't help it. Mother looks just like Robin Hood's desperate Maid Marian when she was surrounded by the bad guys.

"Oh, what a shame," Mother repeats over and over, and finally, "No, you really can't come. Yes, I understand. Yes, I am sure I'll find everything I need. Mrs. Takahashi will be here any minute. Don't worry about a thing."

Everything about Mother looks a mess. Her dress is an old one, rarely out of the closet. Food splotches decorate her pale green apron. Even her hair looks strange with curls springing out in every direction.

She's been working on this dinner for days now. Dinner parties aren't unusual for the Griffin house, but this one is different. Mother explained why yesterday while Polly helped her unpack yet another box of groceries delivered to the back door.

"You see, Polls, all of Father's colleagues from the English Department are coming." Half listening, Polly watches where Mother puts the bar of baking chocolate. Even though it's bitter, she loves taking little nibbles on the sly. "This is the year they decide if Father will be promoted to full professor. Everything has to be perfect."

But something is wrong with Mrs. Hastings. This is bad. Mother is a terrible cook.

Slowly replacing the hearing piece, Mother spots her. "Oh Polly, I'm really going to need your help. Dear me! Why does Mrs. Hastings have to be sick, today of all days?"

Polly has seen Mother look this miserable once

before: when she lost that tennis match to Mrs. Hiller, the worst player at the club.

So, rather than having an adventure at the creek, Polly, Jerry, and Tori are Mother's slaves. That's how Polly sees their working on a miserably hot day when they could be cool and happy in the creek. First they have to collect all of Father's books scattered around the house. Then, while Polly sweeps, Jerry and Tori hose down the front steps and walkway. Those accidental sprays from the hose almost make it fun.

Cutting the white calla lilies growing along the shady side of the house is OK, mostly because they can hide from Mother. After each of Polly's snips, Tori places a long-stemmed flower in the basket.

"Say, Polly, did ya see me helping Professor Cole move into our building this week?" Jerry asks from atop the nearby stone wall. "He gave me a nickel."

"Not a wooden one, I'll bet," Tori teases.

"Naw, but he said he'd help me with my wireless receiver. He knows about stuff like that."

Polly looks up at Jerry banging the heels of his scuffed-up brown shoes against the stone wall. A tan cap sits low on his head, making his ears look larger than ever. His pants barely reach his knees. Something's different. He's skinnier, but that's not it. Then she knows—he's so cheery, positively happy. She sure hopes this doesn't have to do with that icky moment in the moving picture show. No, that couldn't be it. That silly smile of his must have something to do with his precious wireless.

"By the way," he goes on, "I've been thinking about that note you sent last night, Polly. The bucket-phone bumped the window kinda hard, but Mom didn't hear."

"What'd you say?" Tori asks.

"Oh, I just asked him if he wants to carry the charm around for a while. Do you, Jerry?"

"You bet!"

"Great! It's not working for me, and I didn't let go of it for a minute. Maybe you'll have better luck."

"Your wish didn't come true, huh? Wetherbys still here?" he asks with a big grin. Polly knows her friends don't believe in her wish coming true, but she doesn't mind the teasing.

"OK, Mr. Smarty. What's your wish going to be?"

"Oh, I don't know. Really haven't thought much about it," he replies vaguely.

"What about you, Tori, when it's your turn?" Polly asks.

"I'm not sure. I've been thinking that my wish'll be something for the three of us — something we can keep forever. My biggest problem is deciding where to hide the nickel. My brothers are so nosy they get into everything."

Polly takes the coin from her pocket.

"OK, Mr. Berman. Off the wall and on your knees!"

Jerry laughs but obediently kneels on the grass just the way knights do for their queens. He looks up at Polly, smiling.

Her chin slightly raised, Polly uses her most majestic voice. "Jerry Berman, I hereby give you this precious gem to protect with your life. May all your wishes come true." Tapping his head with one of the long-stemmed flowers, she continues. "Arise now and accept this as a token of my trust in you."

Polly is satisfied. Ceremonies are important. Tori and Jerry must feel the same; they never refuse to play along.

"Oh, I almost forgot," she says after scrambling to the top of the wall, squeezing in between Jerry and Tori. The cool stones feel good against her bare legs. "Smilin' Sam was at our house this week! I just came home from school and there he was, walking away. He didn't see me."

"What'd he want?" Jerry asks.

"Don't know. Mother was at tennis so he talked with Mrs. Hastings."

One look at Jerry's scowl tells Polly his doubts about Smilin' Sam just got bigger. Jerry can be such a worry-wart.

"When I asked her what Smilin' Sam wanted, she

just gave me a disgusted look and said she sent him on his way. Poor guy."

"Yeah, but don't you think it's strange he picked this street to visit, of all streets?" Jerry asks. "I don't think it's a coincidence, Polly. I think he knew just where you lived."

"Maybe he wanted to say hello. He wouldn't . . . "

" . . . do anything wrong?" Tori says, finishing Polly's sentence. The question hangs in the air.

Mother's shout breaks the silence.

"Polly! Finished yet?"

"Yes, Mother. Here we come," she calls back, looking at the half-filled basket of flowers.

After lunch there is more to do—shucking the corn is OK, but shelling peas is more fun. Besides, Mother will never notice the missing ones. Polly picks the top step of the porch for this job, hoping a breeze will find them. While they pop open the shells, Polly tells Tori and Jerry about her new favorite book, *The Little Princess*.

What she doesn't tell them is how she likes to imagine herself as the little princess in the story; how maybe her mother and father adopted her, unaware she is really a princess. They just haven't yet learned the truth.

"So, the poor little girl, who was treated so badly by all these mean people, was really a princess after all!"

"I'll bet her father was sorry he lost track of her," Jerry says.

Polly is just about to tell about the happy reunion of father and daughter, her favorite part of the book. Busy shelling peas and talking, she is surprised to hear someone say her name.

"Polly Griffin."

She looks up. Agnes Wetherby is at the bottom of the steps.

"Well, isn't this cute. Helping mommy, are we, oddballs?"

Polly freezes. Then, not wanting to seem too rude, she mumbles a hello. Jerry and Tori stay quiet.

As usual Agnes looks perfect; all in white and cool as ice. Polly stares at Agnes's shoe resting on the porch step; white, clean, and more suited for church than play.

"Well, let's see who's here. We have Miss Polly Perfect, and Mister Jerry Jerk." Then, looking directly at Tori, Agnes adds, "Ah, but your friend here, the maid's little girl. Funny, I can't seem to recall your name, though you seem to be here all the time."

"I've already told you, Agnes. This is Tori," Polly says while frantically thinking of a good name for Agnes, one that would hurt back. "Tori, meet Miss Agnes . . . Miss Agnes . . . Nothing's-Ever-Good-Enough-For-Me-Smarty-Pants!"

There, that'll show her. Agnes is always snotty to Jerry and worse to Tori. That scene at the glove counter with Mrs. Berman had to be the worst.

"Your friend? Amazing! The next thing you know, little Miss Tori and her family will want to move into our neighborhood. You do know it's against the law, don't you, Miss Tori?" Agnes raises her eyebrows so high they nearly touch the brim of her lavender sun hat.

Polly doesn't answer back. She can't. Agnes isn't making any sense.

"Frankly, I think it's a good law," Agnes goes on. "Why, if we let one Japanese family move into our neighborhood, the others will follow. They could take over everything. *The yellow peril*, that's what my father calls them."

"That's the stupidest thing I ever heard," Polly says.

"Are you calling my father stupid? I'm sure he'd like to hear about that. In fact, I think I'll go tell him right now, that you called him stupid!"

"You're the stupid one, Agnes," Polly replies, her throat tight with anger. "If Tori and her family want to live in our neighborhood, they can. After all, it's a free country, isn't it?"

"Yes Polly," Agnes says in a syrupy, sweet voice. "Free for some." Looking at Tori she adds, "But not for everyone! It's the law, you know."

"There's no law like that, Agnes. You're just being

mean," Polly says, now standing, hands planted on her hips.

"Oh, yes, there is! Ask your little friend here. She'll tell you all about it. Won't you, Tori? You really don't belong here, do you! Well, good day Miss Perfect and Mister Jerk."

Spinning around, Agnes walks away. Polly doesn't know what to say. She looks at Jerry. He is squeezing his cap into a shapeless lump. Tori, chin touching her chest, holds a half-emptied pea pod.

Polly can't speak. It's as if when Agnes left she took Polly's voice with her. But so many thoughts race through her head. Laws? Laws that keep people like the Takahashis from living in her neighborhood?

"Tori?"

"Forget her, Polly. She's just mean," Tori says.

Polly doesn't know what to do. Agnes's words were too terrible. Jerry breaks the silence.

"Miss Agnes Smarty Mouth," he says.

Polly likes this. "No, Miss Agnes The Most Horrible. Why, she's the most horrible person I know! Besides, she's stupid! Where did Miss Stupid Agnes ever come up with such a dumb idea?"

"Ignore her," Tori says.

A shout from inside the house keeps Polly from coming up with another Agnes name for the growing list.

"Children! Done with those peas yet?"

"A few more minutes, Mother! We'll bring them right in," Polly yells back.

Quickly, she begins shelling the last few. Wordlessly, Jerry and Tori help. Polly hates the silence.

"Say, Tori, I've been thinking."

"Oh, oh," Jerry snorts, "Watch out Tori. Polly's been thinking."

"No, really. Listen to me. I'm certain Agnes made that up. There can't be laws like that. I'm right, aren't I?"

Tori is so quiet, Polly can hear a bunch of dry leaves dancing down the street, pushed along by a gusty breeze.

"Well, aren't I?"

"Polly Griffin," Tori says, her bottom lip quivering, tears filling her eyes. "You don't know anything, either! Sometimes I think you're just as stupid as Agnes!"

"But I—"

"No, just stop! Stay out of this. It's none of your business!"

"I only—"

"Just stay out of this!"

Tori grabs the bowl of peas from Polly's lap, and heads inside. Polly and Jerry follow.

The kitchen counter and table are covered with

bowls and platters. All the cabinet doors are ajar. Mrs. Takahashi is standing at the sink peeling potatoes. Mother is tearing up bits of parsley for waiting platters.

"Finally!" Mother says, taking the bowl from Tori. Then, with a half smile, "What would I have done without all of you?" After brushing a few stray curls from her forehead with the back of her hand, she reaches for her purse. "Look, I've run out of paprika. My deviled eggs will look very sad without it. Please, one last thing. I promise. Will you go to the store for me? Here's three pennies, one for each of you. You've certainly earned a nice treat."

"If it's OK, Mrs. Griffin, I think I'll stay here," Tori says. "I want to see that book you were talking about, Polly — *The Little Princess*."

Oddly, Polly is relieved. Seconds ago Tori was as angry as a hornet. Polly doesn't want to be stung again. But then, Tori never goes to the store with them. Come to think of it, Tori doesn't go to lots of places with them. That's when Polly gets a truly terrible idea. Maybe Agnes is right. Maybe there are laws about the Japanese that say what they can and cannot do.

Chapter Eight

❦ Tori ❦

Tori found Polly's book sitting on one of the piles they had moved to the Professor's study. Clutching the book to her chest, she walked unnoticed through the chaos of the kitchen to the quiet of the bamboo garden. She really wasn't interested in reading, not now. But the book gave her an excuse to be alone, away from everyone.

As soon as she entered the hidden middle of the grove, the quiet encircled her. The plaid blanket was still there. Time to think—that's what she needed.

Miss Agnes Who Doesn't Know What She's Talking About and Never Will! That's what Tori would've said to her face, if she could have. But Agnes's words hurt as if a thousand arrows had pierced her chest.

Some of what Agnes said she'd already heard, usually late at night when she was supposed to be sleeping. In hushed voices Mama and Papa would talk, mostly in the living room, sometimes at the kitchen table. Tori would lay quietly in bed, her little brothers fast asleep. She'd stare at the beam of light shining through the half-closed bedroom door.

Mama might say something like, "I walked by a pretty little house for sale today. It's not too far from the nursery."

"Uh-huh," Papa would say.

"It has three bedrooms and two bathrooms."

"Uh-huh."

"I think we can afford this one," she would say.

"It would probably not work out," Papa would say.

"There are three trees in the front yard."

"Sachiko," Papa would finally say softly, "you know we can't do that."

"The Law," she'd say.

"Yes, the Law," he'd answer.

Or other times Papa would say something like, "Mr. Carlson thinks I made some good purchases this month. He was pleased."

"I am not surprised," Mama would say. "You are a good nursery-man and a good business-man."

"I have been thinking a lot about seeds lately, Sachiko. I think growing seeds for vegetables could be a profitable business. I wouldn't need much land to make it work."

There would be a pause. Then Mama would say, "But we can't do that yet, can we?"

"No Sachiko, not yet. But someday we will. Someday."

Mama and Papa didn't seem worried or upset during these talks. She knew they saved every extra penny they earned. The money would help. The part she didn't understand was when they talked about the Law. Still, when Tori listened to Mama and Papa she wasn't worried either. They'd find a way out of this. They always did.

Now their words held a new and frightening meaning. Tori realized how the laws were meant to hurt her, her family, and her neighbors. People had made these laws to keep her family and other Japanese from choosing where they lived. Were there other laws that kept Papa from owning his own business? Who made these laws? Who thought these laws were a good idea? The Wetherbys seemed to like them. But who else?

At that instant Tori knew she couldn't face Polly and Jerry when they came back from the store. She didn't want to hear Polly go on about awful Agnes this and nasty Agnes that. She didn't want Jerry to look at her in that kindly, knowing way of his. She just wanted to be away from Spruce Street; the Griffins' huge, chaotic house; and the terrible possibility that she really wasn't as welcome as she had always believed. She didn't want to see Polly ever again!

Her stomach hurt. She touched her forehead in the way Mama would be sure to do in the next few minutes when Tori walked into the kitchen to announce she didn't feel very well.

Back in the kitchen, Mama's light touch on her forehead was all it took. Mama and Mrs. Griffin looked worried.

"Oh, she has a fever," Mrs. Griffin said, after feeling Tori's forehead with the back of her cool hand, then peering into her eyes. "I wonder if it's the same bug bothering Mrs. Hastings?"

Tori looked at Mama. Was she thinking about Haruo, Kenji, and Yoshi? When one of the Takahashi children got sick, the others were soon to follow. Poor Mama.

"You've been a great help," Mrs. Griffin said to Mama. "I don't think I could have done any of this without you. Please take Tori home now. My sister will be here to help any minute now."

Mama bowed slightly. Mrs. Griffin continued to chatter. Tori had been around Mrs. Griffin long enough to know that being excited made her talkative, just like it did for Polly.

"The only thing left to do is bake the mystery cake, Bernard's favorite. My sister, Charlotte, is on her way with the recipe. She'll help. Take Tori home now. We'll be fine."

Now Tori's tummy felt worse. At first she thought she'd just imagined not feeling well. Could pretending do that? How surprising. She had no time to sort it out. Within a few short minutes, she and Mama were on their way out the door. As soon as they arrived at the corner, the bright orange streetcar arrived.

Chapter Nine

❀ Polly ❀

The walk to the store takes longer than usual. Polly doesn't feel like hurrying, or talking either. Jerry is quiet, too. Halfway there, Polly blurts out, "Can you imagine Agnes saying such terrible things? Why, she's got to be the nastiest person I know. She makes up the most hateful stories."

"She's nasty, all right," Jerry nods. "But what she said, about how the Japanese can't live here, it could be true."

Polly is surprised. How does Jerry know this?

"See, Mom reads the newspaper to me almost every morning. I eat, she reads. She can get pretty worked up, too, like when she reads the things folks write about Orientals."

"Orientals?"

"You know, people from Japan and China."

"What sort of things?"

"I don't get a lot of it, but I can tell you, she's plenty upset about these laws."

"But, Jerry, why in the world make laws like these?"

"Shoot, Polly, I don't know."

That's when Polly realizes another terrible thing. These laws mean that Tori will never live next to her.

"This is all a bunch of hateful lies, Jerry! Why would you tell me such stories?"

"I'm not, honest!"

"I thought you were my friend. Friends don't go around saying this."

"Look, I'm just telling you what my mom says."

"Well, you've just got to be wrong!" Then she says the worst thing she can think of. "You sound just like Agnes!"

Jerry scowls. Quickening his pace, he walks several steps ahead of her. Polly can't blame him. She's being horrible, but she can't help it. What a miserable day! She hurries to catch up.

"Sorry, Jer," she mumbles.

"S'OK."

He kicks a large chestnut into the street before he says anything else. "This Japanese stuff is giving me a headache." Pushing his cap to the back of his head, he says, "Until Agnes, I never really thought about Tori being Japanese."

The Bamboo Garden

Almost at the grocery store, Polly remembers something. Tori never comes here with them, even though she loves candy. She always finds an excuse. Could Tori feel funny here, kind of like an outsider? Minutes later Polly leaves the store with a jar of paprika and three extra-long licorice ropes in a paper bag. She doesn't say much; there's a lot to sort out.

I'm going to do something. Tori was really mad at me for talking about it. But I've just got to find a way to make things better for her. I've got to. None of this is fair! Tori is my best friend in the whole world. I'd do anything for her.

"Pols, where's the paprika? What took you so long? Oh, I just don't know what to do. This is just a disaster!"

"But, Mother, we hurried!"

"Oh, no, it's not you! It's Tori! Mrs. Takahashi had to take her home. The poor girl seems to have developed a fever. Oh dear, today of all days. What an amazing amount of bad luck!"

Chapter Ten

⸙ Tori ⸙

"Oh, Papa, it's going to be a beautiful bamboo garden. Thank-you for starting on it today."

The gardens in Tori's neighborhood all looked the same—lots of grass and a few young, skinny trees, years away from providing real shade for the small homes. But Papa wanted something different for the Takahashi house. Tori sat on a large flat boulder watching Papa dig. His white shirt was already wet even though he had just started digging. A wide-brimmed straw hat shaded his face from the sun. The blustery breeze did little to cool off the hot September Sunday.

"Bamboo is popular here, Toriko. We can't seem to keep enough on hand for our customers. But I've been saving these just for you," Papa said, freeing the little shoots from their tiny clay pots.

The Bamboo Garden

"Thank-you, Papa."

"I remember the bamboo garden in my parents' home. A breeze like the one we have today would blow through the canes, making everything sound cooler." After another shovel or two he continued talking softly, almost as if Tori weren't there. "In the summer, during the Tanabata Festival, we all wrote our wishes on colored paper and tied them to bamboo branches. The slightest puff of air would lift our wishes to the sky."

"What would you wish for, Papa?" Tori asked, surprised by this new story. More surprising was the idea of Papa making wishes.

"Always the same thing, Toriko—I always hoped I could be more skilled at writing Japanese characters. My teachers had almost given up on me." He sounded embarrassed.

As he spoke Tori heard the lively tinkle of their wind chime encouraged by a strong breeze. Mama had asked him to hang the glass chimes near the kitchen window so she could hear them when she washed dishes. Even though Tori wanted to ask Papa how long it would take for the tiny bamboo sprouts to grow as tall as Polly's, her thought remained unspoken. She would not show her impatience. This morning with Papa was special. She would be careful not to spoil the moment with too many questions.

Luckily, Mama and the boys would be at church for a while. After services, with Yoshi playing nearby Mama and the other women in her sewing circle were sure to be talking about more than stitches. Haruo and Kenji would be at baseball practice, which was more exciting than usual. New uniforms were to be handed out today.

"Toriko, are you sure you're feeling better?" Mama had asked before she left. Tori, sitting up in bed, felt funny about Mama being so concerned. Mama was in a hurry; yet she delayed leaving. She wouldn't go until she'd explained about lunch in the icebox and how Tori could join Papa in the garden.

As soon as Mama left, Tori went outside. She decided that being a little bit sick was just fine because now she had the whole morning to herself and time with Papa. Yesterday's ugly scene at the Griffins' had faded for the moment.

Papa rarely had time to work on their garden. Yet he had transformed the plain grass yard into something special—something Papa said looked like the home he had left in Japan. A mossy boulder here, a low-growing cypress there, a little gravel path, an iron lantern sitting just so, a small pond for water plants and fish. No flowers, just different shades of green.

"I'm planting these young shoots along the back

fence. Soon they will be high enough to create a tall wall of green. I think you had a good idea, Toriko," he said, one knee resting in the rich black soil he had just loosened. "Someday, when I build our tea house back here, we'll be surrounded by great stalks of bamboo."

"Papa, do you ever wish you were back in Japan?"

Papa stopped his digging and looked at Tori. For a few seconds he said nothing.

"Toriko, America is my home now," he finally replied in a low voice.

"But, Papa, I don't think they want us here."

There, she had said it! She didn't mean to. Even though Tori had so far managed to keep the painful conversation with Agnes out of her mind, suddenly it was all there in front of her. Perhaps Papa could help her understand.

"Who are you speaking of?"

"Oh, I don't know. But Papa, is there really a law that says we can't buy a house wherever we want?"

Papa put down his muddied trowel and sat next to Tori. He pulled a white handkerchief from his pocket, folded it neatly into quarters and wiped his wet forehead.

"Well, yes, Toriko. There are laws like that."

"Why are there these laws, Papa?" Tori asked,

realizing her stomachache was back, a dull pain that came and went in waves.

"Toriko, America is a land of opportunity. Look at me. I'm a manager of one of Berkeley's biggest nurseries. Look at our family. We have this lovely home with a garden and nice neighbors. You children are getting a good education. What more could we want?"

"But we can't buy this house, can we?"

"Ah, what you say is true. Mama and I cannot buy this house." He sat quietly, absent-mindedly removing the mud from the trowel with his free hand.

"I don't think that's fair," Tori said, impatient with Papa's silence. "Why do they have laws about us, just because we're Japanese? Don't they want us here?"

"I don't know why, Toriko. But I do know that some people are afraid of us, and they're the ones who make these laws."

"What are they afraid of?"

"I'm not sure I can answer that," he said, shaking his head. He paused for a moment, thoughtful. "I will tell you one thing, Toriko. I do not let any of this bother me."

He stood now, adjusted his hat, and picked up another bamboo plant. Instead of resuming his planting, he smiled.

"What's so funny, Papa?"

"A little thought, Toriko. It goes like this. Some

people are afraid to plant bamboo. They worry that it is so vigorous, it will take over the garden, growing wherever it likes."

Tori got it right away. "Like us, Papa? Do you think the people who make these laws think we're like bamboo, that we might take over their gardens?"

"Yes, I think so!"

Even though Papa's idea didn't make her feel better, it did help to talk about it. Would she ever have the same kind of talk with Polly and Jerry? Up until yesterday she had truly felt like one of Polly's best friends. Today that was no longer true. She didn't belong on Spruce Street, and she never would. She lived on the other side of town. She looked different. She was Japanese-American. Polly and Jerry only saw the Japanese part of her. They had pretended to like her. They were just being nice to the maid's daughter.

Tori wasn't the tiniest bit sorry she had yelled at Polly yesterday. That stupid wish of hers about her family living next door to the Griffins was also pretend. She probably didn't mean it in the first place. Polly has probably made up a new wish by now.

Tori watched Papa put the last bamboo shoot into the dark, moist soil. Then, crouching by the pond, he picked out leaves that had blown over its glassy green surface. Tori looked for the three little fish living there. The two bright orange ones were easy to spot, but the third was harder. Its black-and-white spots made hiding easier in the dark shadows of the water plants. She finally found it with only a bit of white tail showing.

I know what it's like, little fish, Tori thought, helping to pluck out a few soggy leaves. Sometimes your friends don't want you around. Maybe they're not even your friends. They're probably pretending to like you so they have someone to play with. Why, you don't even look like them! They don't know anything about you. Worse yet, they don't care.

That's when she knew what her wish would be if she ever had the chance to hold onto Smilin' Sam's nickel. It wouldn't be like Papa's wish. Tori's was much more important than wanting to write Japanese characters. She'd wish for a real, true friend. A real friend was someone who likes you just the way you are, a real friend to stick up for you. A real friend who would want to know about everything that mattered to you. That certainly wasn't Polly Griffin.

Chapter Eleven

⚘ Polly ⚘

Polly can't help wondering—is Tori really sick or is she just mad? A small part of Polly is relieved Tori left. So much happened—Agnes, their fight, those ugly laws. Her head is spinning. Besides, the rest of the afternoon is "Polly, do this" or "Polly, do that."

Next morning Polly wants to telephone the Takahashis. But she can't. Mother and Father want her to listen to their stories about the party, like how Professor Cole kept everyone in stitches about some of the odd characters he meets, or about how Mrs. Dougherty arrived wearing the exact same dress as Mrs. Polk.

"Polly, this will be good for Mrs. Takahashi. I told everyone who complimented me that she made my dress. It was beautiful, wasn't it, Bernard?"

"Yes, my dear. Beautiful."

"And the food, Bernard. What did you think?"

Next Mother asks Father about every single dish. He has something nice to say about everything.

At last Polly escapes to the telephone. She's ready with questions. Does Tori feel better? Would she like to go to Berkeley Beach with her after church? Jerry's coming, too. The telephone rings and rings. No one answers. Does this mean Tori is better? Polly wants to smooth things over. The scene with Agnes was awful, but the fight with Tori was so much worse. The phone rings and rings, but no one answers. Maybe she's doing homework. Even though school just started, Tori's like that. She doesn't put things off.

The day would have been bunches better if Mother didn't insist that Donald and Millie go along. "I'm just too exhausted for Berkeley Beach today, Polls," Mother says wearily, stretched out on the bedroom's blue velvet chaise lounge, an open book in her lap. Father is stuck in his study as usual.

Playing with Jerry on the wide sandy beach cooled by steady bay breezes helps erase the hot streetcar ride. But every so often, her thoughts turn to Tori.

I always thought Tori didn't like the beach and that's why she never came with us. Now I'm not so sure. Maybe there are other reasons. I don't see other Japanese faces around. Would she feel funny here? Could that be it? I know she'd never feel that way with me. We're best friends, aren't we?

On the streetcar ride home, Donald and Millie sit in the back joking with their university friends. The heat and the rhythmic grinding of the street-car's metal wheels in their iron tracks lull Polly into a sleepy, day-dreamy mood. If Jerry hadn't tapped her on the shoulder, she might have missed their stop.

"Wow, that's blowing hard," Polly hollers as she jumps off the streetcar's wooden step. The frisky bay breeze had become a strong, gusty wind.

"Yeah, but it's still hotter than blazes," Jerry shouts back. "Wouldn't it be fun to sleep on the beach all night? Say, I've got a keen idea! I'm going to spend the night in your hammock."

Polly is sorry she didn't think of it first.

As they near the house, Donald pats Polly's head. "Hey, Little Squirt. Remember your instructions." Then in a perfect imitation of Mother, he orders, "No sand in my house, Polly Griffin. That's why the news-paper's on the laundry room floor. Dust off every speck, then march yourself right upstairs to the bathtub."

Polly exchanges a grin with Jerry and follows him down the driveway to the garden gate. A burst of wind slams the gate shut behind him.

"Bye, Polly!" Jerry shouts. "Don't forget—bring that arrowhead."

Deep in her dress pocket, Polly touches the rock they found on the beach, most definitely an arrowhead. Jerry isn't certain. Maybe her teacher, Miss Lamb, will know.

Polly lazes in her tub of bubbles. The Ivory soap bar is a ship afloat on a stormy sea. If it weren't for the yummy dinner smells drifting under the door, she could have stayed forever. Macaroni-and-cheese aromas eventually lure her out.

"Polly, bring that pitcher of lemonade with you," Mother calls from the garden, "and the basket of silverware, too."

Polly tries not to laugh at Mother frantically wrestling with the red-and-white-checkered tablecloth she tries to hold down. Just as she gets one end settled, the other flies up.

Donald carries the dishes, Millie a giant bowl of salad.

"Bernard!" Mother shouts. "Dinner's ready! Bring the casserole with you on your way out, please!"

Polly looks through the open window into Father's study. He doesn't move. Polly waits for what comes next. Mother will yell one more time before he leaves his desk. It's always that way.

"So, Polly, tell us about your day at the beach," Father asks, when everyone is settled around the table. She knows he's feeling guilty. All summer he's been feverishly working on his book. Only one chapter left. "Have to keep the momentum going," he has told her more than once.

"We dug up an arrowhead in the sand, a real one this time," she boasts.

No one listens. Father's napkin flies across the yard. Millie and Donald are busy holding down a piece of the tablecloth. It keeps flapping noisily, trying to break free. A sudden gust tumbles the rose vase, spilling water onto Mother's plate. Eating outdoors isn't fun anymore. The wind doesn't cool anything. Worst of all, no one wants to hear her arrowhead story.

Standing up, napkin tucked firmly in his waistband, Father makes an announcement. "Come on, everyone. Time to go in! It'll be better inside."

Just then a strong puff snaps Millie's napkin from her hand.

"That's it!" Mother says. "Let's go."

"A real gale-like wind, I'd call it," Father declares.

Glad to be inside, Polly listens to tree limbs and bushes bang against the house. Where would the next thump or bump come from? A steady hammering sound from the back of the house grows louder, more persistent.

"Polly, go take that bucket phone off the rope. We don't want to hear that noise all night."

She runs upstairs to her sunporch. From there she

can see Jerry helping his mother tie up the canvas rolls that hang in the screened part of their apartment. The wind whips the rolls back and forth. After freeing the bucket from the rope, Polly waves to Jerry.

Later, Polly helps Millie dry dishes. When the last cup is stowed away, Polly dashes to the living room. Mother is waiting. With a thump Polly plops next to her, snuggling under her arm. Tonight Father is reading the most exciting part of *The Arabian Nights,* about Aladdin's first ride on the magic carpet.

Polly is convinced Father is the most dramatic reader in all of Berkeley, the way he waves his hands in the air and how his voice rises to a shout or falls to a whisper. His bushy eyebrows bouncing up and down are especially fun to watch as he reads. She loves the story, especially the magic carpet part.

Father is telling about how the wind whips across Aladdin's face as he sits cross-legged on his brightly colored rug. *Bang! Bang! Bang!* He stops reading.

"For heaven's sake, what is that?" Mother exclaims.

Father slams the book shut.

"Sounds like one of our trash can lids took off. Hope it's not the one with the ashes in it. Donald, take a look, please."

When Donald returns, his usually slicked-down hair is almost standing straight up. Patting it back into place, he tells everyone what happened.

"By jingo, that wind is really something! The lid was halfway down the block by the time I caught up with it!"

"Pretty strong to do that," Father says, putting the book down. "Well, let's just call it a night. Got to catch the early morning ferry to San Francisco. Date with my publisher. He wants to see the manuscript. Hope he likes it. Polly, tie down those canvas rolls of yours. They're bound to make a racket."

Slowly Polly drags herself upstairs. Even though her homework is finished, she has those Sunday-night-before-school butterflies. Making a "good-bad" list helps. After drawing a line down the middle of her paper, she writes GOOD on one side with a green crayon and BAD on the other in red. On the GOOD side she puts Berkeley Beach, and the dinner party, which made Mother and Father happy. From her secret place at the top of the stairs, she had a great view, especially of Professor Cole. He'd come by himself, but in no time there was a crowd around him, laughing a lot. On the BAD side, she'd have to put that Agnes business, in capital letters, underlined in red, blue, and purple! Tori yelled at her. That wasn't good. Of course all that business Jerry said about the laws — that had to be the WORST.

The wind keeps up its huffing and puffing by the time she's in bed. She's sleepy but the warm, blustery evening leaves her restless. Agnes's spiteful words to Tori keep shoving their way into her head.

Your friend? Amazing! Japanese in our neighborhood? That's not allowed. Let one in, more will come, take over everything. You'll see. The yellow peril.

Even with all the banging and slamming going on in the house, Polly can hear Father switch off her bedroom light.

"Father! Is that you?" she yells from the sleeping porch.

"Yes, Polly." He stands in the doorway. "Come on, young lady. It's a school night. You should be asleep by now."

"I know, Father. It's just that I can't. It's awfully noisy. Would you fix my sheets, please?"

Polly hates when her bottom sheet gets crinkly. Mother and Father never refuse her request. Father pulls the sheet tight, wrinkles gone. Then he sits down on her bed, just as she hoped.

"Father, I've got a really important question to ask you. It's probably the most important question I've ever asked in my whole life!"

"Well, if it's that important, I guess you'd better ask. What's up, Miss Griffin?"

She tells Father what she knows about those laws and can tell he's paying close attention because of all his "uh-huh" and "yes, I understand" noises.

"Is it true, Father? If the Takahashis want to move next door to us, they can't?"

"Yes, I'm afraid it is, dear girl."

"Isn't there anything we can do about it?"

"Sorry to say, I don't think so. But that doesn't mean for one second that Mother and I think these laws are good. You do know that, don't you?" Even in the dark, Polly knows Father is frowning.

"Yes, sir."

Father's words don't make her feel better. In fact, something about the way he said there was nothing to be done frightens her. Throwing off her quilt, Polly wraps herself in the cool cotton sheet. She didn't expect Tori to be gone when she got back from the store. Tori was hardly ever sick. Maybe the licorice rope will help. She'll give it to Mrs. Takahashi on her Tuesday cleaning day.

Even though she tied up the canvas rolls, they still thump noisily. Wind howls as it races around the house. Catches and locks on all the doors and windows bang and rattle. Every time Polly drifts off, something shakes, clatters, or bumps. When sleep finally arrives, it doesn't last long. Clanging bells and screaming sirens jar her awake. Polly races across the hall to her parents' bedroom. Mother and Father are also up.

"This is serious, dear," Father says as he pulls

on a pair of pants over his pajama bottoms. "A fire and a strong wind mean trouble. What do you think, Mother? Don't you think I should see what's happening?"

Polly doesn't wait to hear the answer. She dashes back to the sleeping porch for her robe and shoes. If Father is going out to see a fire, she will, too!

Of course, she isn't sure Father will say yes, but she wants to be ready just in case. Tying her other shoe, Polly hears Father going downstairs. Donald's with him, his long-legged footsteps skipping every other stair.

"Father, please! Let me go, too," Polly shouts, throwing the robe over her nightgown as she runs to catch up. "I'll be careful. I'll stay with you. I just want to see what's happening."

Normally, Father would never agree to such a thing. But Polly hopes he still feels guilty about not going to the beach. She also knows Father loves an adventure, especially the storytelling part afterward.

"Please, Father!"

"Very well. But stay close. We'll only go to see the fire, then come right back. No one's going to sleep through this racket anyhow."

The night air is hot and dry, the wind so strong Polly leans into it as they walk up Cedar Street. She hears sirens up ahead. Curious neighbors come out of their homes. Polly almost laughs aloud at how funny they look. Several of them stand under the glow of their porch lamps, robes askew and nightcaps resting on sleep-mussed hair. She tightens the belt on her own bathrobe as she tries to keep up with Father. He looks grim.

"Father, are you worried?" Polly asks, wanting him to say no.

Father surprises her. "Yep, Polly, I am. We do love our shake-shingled houses. You know as well as I—fire is the enemy of all that wood." Before this moment, Polly didn't think about how these big homes would feed a fire. For an instant she pictures all of them aflame, lighting the night sky with a red-and-orange glow. She quickly erases the idea from her mind.

It's hard walking uphill. Finally, at the corner of Euclid and Cedar, she knows she won't have to go any farther. Three fire trucks carrying either hoses or ladders are lined up. The pumper truck is also there, sending up plumes of white steam from its smokestack. Lots of firemen are holding on to hoses aimed at a two-story wood-frame building.

"Hey!" Donald shouts above the noise. "That's the Dwight Club! I have pals living there!"

Several young men are standing in the street. He runs ahead to join them. A small part of the roof is on fire. From where Polly stands, it looks like the firemen are winning the battle. The red-orange flames get smaller and smaller. A few more minutes of soaking turns the flames into a plume of white smoke curling into the black night sky.

"Well, that's a relief," Father says, his words nearly lost in a passing gust of wind. "Wouldn't take much for those cinders to fly around. No telling what that would lead to."

On the way home, the streets are nearly deserted. Porch lights turned off, the neighborhood is dark and spooky. The fire is no longer a threat, but the howl of that unrelenting wind seems almost as bad.

Polly reaches for Father's large, warm hand. Gently, he gives her a squeeze.

"Polly, I think I should share a little secret with you."

"A secret!"

"Righto! But this will be our little secret. How's that sound?"

"I think that'd be just raspberries, Father!"

"You see, Polly, I happen to know something about those laws you mentioned earlier, perhaps a little more than I let on. Shall I tell you what I know?"

"Oh, yes please, Father."

He clears his throat before going on, just the way Polly imagines he does in class before one of his lectures. She hopes it isn't going to be boring, but how could a secret ever be boring?

"Now, it is true that Tori's father and mother will not be able to buy a house, or any property, for that matter. But now, here's the secret part. As I understand it, there are ways around this problem. Are you with me?"

"Yes, sir," she says with growing excitement.

"It's simple, actually. Now let's see. Tori and her brothers were born here, right?"

"Yes, sir."

"Well, what does that make them?"

Oh, no! Father's playing teacher! This might go on forever. Why can't he just get to the point? But, she'd better go along with it or she'll never hear the secret.

"What do you mean, Father?"

"Think about it. When people are born in this country, that means they are . . . "

Father waits for her to finish his sentence. What does he want her to say? Think, Polly, think! Father is quiet. *If someone is born in this country this means they are what?* Wait, that's it!

"American citizens!" she shouts.

"That's right. Now, as I understand it, this law says that folks like the Takahashis can't buy property, mainly because they're not citizens. Right?"

"I guess so."

"Now comes the secret. Ready?"

"Ready."

"Tori can!"

"Tori can what?"

"Buy property!"

"Father, what are you talking about? Tori doesn't even have enough money to go to the moving picture show with me!"

Polly is crushed. Here she thought Father would have the answer, but he's only talking in riddles.

"Listen to me, Polly. Here's how it works. Mr. and Mrs. Takahashi buy property in Tori's name. That means Tori is the owner, but not really. It's her parents' money. It's just her name on the contract, nice and legal. Get it? It's done all the time. It's called a 'loophole' and it works."

Relief sweeps over Polly. Of course! As easy as pie! Tori's just got to hear this. But wait—if it's a secret, how can she tell Tori?

"Father," she says, squeezing his hand extra tight, "this is the best secret I've ever heard. But, please, may I share it with Tori? I know it'd make her feel oodles better. Please, Father?"

"I suppose so. Legal loopholes aren't the usual kind of secret. Now, let's talk about something even more important."

Polly can't imagine anything more important than

the loophole, but from the sound of his voice, she knows that by the time they walk into the house, they are sure to have an amazing story to tell. After they make Mother laugh about how Donald saves Berkeley from destruction, Polly will add something to her list. On the GOOD side she'll print, in extra large letters: THE LOOPHOLE. But when can she tell Tori? Certainly not now. No matter how exciting her news, Polly doubts that a telephone call at two o'clock in the morning would make anyone very happy.

Chapter Twelve

❦ Polly ❦

Even with closed eyes, Polly knows something is different. No familiar smell of bacon in the pan or coffee on the stove. Instead, the spicy scent of burning leaves floats into her sleeping porch—probably the Wetherby gardener getting an early start. Last night's adventure makes it hard to get up. Pulling the sheet over her head, Polly snuggles in for a few extra winks.

"Polly! Are you dressed?"

Mother's shout puts an abrupt halt to this idea. Throwing off the covers, Polly swings her feet onto the cool wood floor.

"Come on! These eggs aren't going to wait forever!"

By the time Polly is downstairs, there is only one thing on her mind. *The loophole!* She'll call Tori right after school. Father must have been up extra early.

He's gone, but the newspaper is open to the funnies, something they usually read together. That's when she remembers his appointment in San Francisco.

"Now Polly, come home right before lunch," Mother says, putting Polly's breakfast plate in front of her. Nibbling the slightly burned bacon, Polly watches Mother write on her good stationery with perfect letters and no ink splotches. She talks as she writes. "I'll have a sandwich ready for you in the icebox. You can eat it on the way."

"Yes, Mother."

"We've got to be at Dr. Wright's at twelve forty-five, so no dawdling. Here, you'll need this for your teacher."

Mother carefully blots the note, then tucks it into Polly's dress pocket. Ugh, her visit to the dentist. That's definitely going on the BAD side of her list. Still, she is getting out of school early.

Mother is already dressed for tennis. The white blouse and long skirt look cool on this already hot morning. Her sun visor is in place, scrunching down her blond curls. Helen Wills, the US Women's Tennis Champion, is going to conduct a special class just for Mother and the other tennis club ladies.

"Polls, I'll be back from the club by the time you get home. Now finish that orange juice. I don't want to see one drop left in your glass."

Drat! If only Mother forgot this is cod-liver-oil day. But that never happens! Holding her nose sometimes helps, but not always. As she swallows the fishy, smelly drink, she can't help wondering how it can be good for you. It makes her feel sick.

The wind slams the front door behind her at the very moment Jerry runs across the front lawn.

"Hi, Jerry," she shouts above the noisy, blustery wind.

"You got the arrowhead, Polly?" he shouts back, holding his cap with one hand, his black metal lunch pail with the other.

"Oh, gee, Jerry, I forgot. I'm sorry. I'll bring it tomorrow."

He seems disappointed.

On their walk to school, Polly talks the whole way about the fire. But she can't help noticing something strange. Houses, trees, even shrubs seem extra bright, kind of like looking at the world through a newly washed window.

By the time she gets to school, Polly has told Jerry all about the fire and how Donald helped his buddies. The school bell interrupts her. "I'll tell you more this afternoon, like how Mr. and Mrs. Anderson looked in their matching pajamas. What a hoot!" She also reminds herself to tell him about the loophole.

Sliding onto the cool wood bench of her desk feels

good. How can it be this hot so early in the morning? That pesky wind didn't cool her in the least. The hours drag by. The hands of the clock will never make it to 12. To make matters worse, Miss Lamb seems more nervous than usual, fiddling with those pearls she always wears and constantly looking out the window.

When noon arrives, Polly waves good-bye to the kids as they grab their lunch boxes from the shelf in the cloakroom. They don't notice. Or are they just pretending they don't see her? Invisible, that's how she feels at school. She can't help feeling smug about leaving the whole bunch of them behind.

The pesky wind makes the walk home slow going. Little specks of dust blow into her eyes. She rubs them away. The smell of burning leaves is annoying. But where are those smoldering piles?

As she turns the corner from Vine onto Spruce Street, Polly is surprised to see several clusters of her neighbors, mainly the women, talking to one another on front porches or sidewalks. Every now and then, they stop midsentence to sniff the air, like Fudge does when Polly puts a juicy carrot in front of her nose.

Bits of conversations float her way.

"Well, I'll tell you what. I'm starting to get worried. This heat and wind, and that fire last night."

"Do you think it's another fire? I'm sure I saw smoke blowing down from the hills."

"Strange. We hardly ever have a wind blowing from there. Usually it comes off the bay."

"Haven't seen one of those bay breezes for ages now."

"Never thought I'd miss our cold, foggy summers."

To Polly's amazement, her mother is in one of these groups in front of their house. She doesn't even notice Polly. Odder yet, one of the ladies standing with Mother is dreadful Mrs. Wetherby. Mother and Mrs. Wetherby rarely talk to each other. Polly can't miss seeing that Mrs. Wetherby's dress buttons aren't done right. How unusual for a woman who likes everything just so.

When Polly gets close enough to hear, the ladies stop talking. Their heads swivel in the same direction. Several red fire trucks race up Spruce Street. Clanging bells and honking horns grow louder and louder, then dim as they rush by. Polly removes her fingers from her ears.

Mother sees her. "Oh, there you are! Good! Run into the house and get your lunch. I'll be here."

"Well, Mrs. Griffin," Mrs. Wetherby continues, deliberately ignoring Polly, "I'm really not the least bit alarmed. After all, it's probably nothing more than our fire company can handle."

While Polly skips to the kitchen, two more fire trucks speed by, rattling all the windows. Inside, things are quieter and cool. Fudge is napping under the kitchen table. Polly is glad she left the pink blanket there this morning, Fudge's favorite. A half-eaten lettuce leaf sits nearby. Goody! Ol' Fudge is eating again. Polly tries to pick her up, but Fudge kicks hard, wiggles free, and scoots back to the pink blanket. Why'd she do that, Polly wonders. It's almost like she's frightened of me. She's never done that before.

New sirens distract Polly. Snatching a brown paper bag from the metal shelf of the icebox, Polly skips back outside, not wanting to miss anything.

Surprisingly, everything is different. Huge black clouds now block out most of the morning sun. The world is dark and gloomy. Polly runs to Mother's side.

"Polls, I've changed my mind. We're not going. Sit on the porch and eat your lunch." Mother's face has lost its usual rosy glow. "There must be a large fire in the hills. We're not going anywhere until I'm satisfied it's staying there."

From the top step of her porch, Polly has a great view of everything on Spruce Street. Most of the ladies and the few men at home talk quietly as they keep watch on the black smoke. Two more fire engines race by, bells ringing loudly. Happy about missing school, Polly pops the last morsel of her baloney sandwich into her mouth. This Monday is turning out to be swell after all.

Almost finished with her apple, Polly hears the Campanile bells begin to clang. Sometimes she can barely hear the bells in the tall tower on campus, but today the sound is clear and loud. Only one o'clock, but strangely the bells go on and on and on. At about the same time, Jerry comes running down the street, along with a few other kids from the neighborhood. Why aren't they in school, she wonders. Maybe the school burnt down. Wouldn't that be the bee's knees?

"Hey, Jerry!" she shouts. "What're you doing home?"

"Oh, they let us out, all of us!" he shouts back. "They're worried about the fire. Told us to go home." Just as he makes the turn up the Griffins' walkway, Mrs. Wetherby snags him by the collar, knocking off his cap.

"What's this all about, young man?" she asks sternly. "What do you mean they let you out of school?"

"Why yes, ma'am, they did." Quickly, he picks up his cap and dusts it off. "It's a big fire, I guess. Anyhow, why don't you ask Agnes?" He points up the street.

Sure enough, there she is, pulling her little brother and sister along behind her. Polly always feels sorry for them, especially now. Agnes yanks their hands. Tommy and Elizabeth struggle to keep up.

Jerry runs up the front steps and plops down next

to Polly before wiping his sweaty forehead with the back of his hand. For a second Polly is a teensy bit annoyed that she isn't the only one out of school. Then she is sad the school didn't burn down. But having Jerry being here is keen. Maybe he'll know why the Campanile bells are ringing.

"Hmmm, could have something to do with the fire," he guesses, "but that doesn't make any sense."

"Why?"

"Well, all the fire trucks are going up into these hills, nowhere near campus."

"Yeah, I guess you're right. Hey, want one of my snickerdoodles?"

Sitting next to Jerry like this, munching cookies, reminds Polly of being at the moving pictures. Only this show is real, so definitely more exciting.

Without warning Mrs. Wetherby steps off the curb into the middle of the street. A fast-moving car squeals to a stop. When Polly opens her eyes, Mrs. Wetherby is still standing, hands on her hips, looking menacingly at the driver who turns out to be a policeman.

"Young man, I demand to know what is going on around here," she bellows.

The policeman's face turns sheet white. As he gets out of the car, Polly sees him take a big breath.

"Good afternoon, ladies."

"Young man, answer my question. What is happening?"

"You see, it's like this. We've got a big grass fire in progress. It's coming from Wildcat Canyon."

The women gasp.

"But don't you worry. We'll have it under control soon. 'Course, this wind doesn't help much. It's — oops!"

He doesn't finish his sentence. A big blast of air grabs his hat, sending it down the street.

"Mother! Ask him about the Campanile." Those ringing bells puzzle Polly most.

When he returns with his hat, now pushed down firmly over his ears, Polly listens as Mother asks the question but only after Mrs. Wetherby first lectures the policeman on being more careful with city property.

"Young man, just remember. Hats don't grow on trees."

From the look on his face, Polly knows he'd like to say something he might be sorry about later. The policeman turns to Mother.

"Seems like a fire is goin' on above campus, too, up in Strawberry Canyon, ma'am. Lots of students fighting that one. The bells are raising the alarm," he says and returns to his police car.

The Bamboo Garden

"Well, there. You see?" Mrs. Wetherby snorts. "Our fire department is taking care of everything. There's nothing to worry about. I told you so!"

She clutches Tommy's and Elizabeth's hands and heads to their house. All this time the two waited quietly on the sidewalk, watching everything, little carbon copies of their big sister. Agnes marches in after them after looking over her shoulder at Polly and Jerry with a long, rude stare.

Polly isn't scared, but that darkening sky is weird. The sun is now completely hidden behind black clouds. Little bits of powdery ash settle on her face and shoulders. The Campanile stops clanging, but other noises take over—fire engine motors, bells, sirens, and powerful wind gusts rushing through the trees.

"Hey, look who's coming!" Polly yells, pointing down the street, hardly believing her eyes. Walking briskly hand-in-hand are Tori and Mrs. Takahashi. Their free hands hold onto their hats, skirts puffing out with every new gust of wind. What could they be doing here, she wonders. Mrs. Takahashi never comes on Mondays. Why isn't Tori in school? Is she still sick? Something isn't right. But what?

Chapter Thirteen

❦ Tori ❦

Tori hated Monday mornings. School was OK but not the getting-out-of-bed part. Things were different that Monday. She was dressed and in the kitchen before Haruo and Kenji opened their eyes.

"Mama, please let me go," Tori begged a third time, as she watched Mama rinse the last few breakfast dishes. "It's the school spelling bee. I've been practicing for weeks."

"No, not today."

"But Mama . . ."

"Maybe tomorrow. You still are not eating right. For now, you must stay home."

"I'm just not hungry, Mama. Besides, there's nothing to do here."

"You can help me with Yoshi. He is a problem these days. That little walk to Tamaro's Grocery takes forever. He won't let me carry him. When we get there, he wants everything he sees. Then he cries when I say no."

"I'll watch him for you, Mama."

Tori didn't mind taking care of Yoshi. Besides, he'd keep her busy. No time to think about things. Talking with Papa had helped, yet thoughts of Polly and Jerry made her feel sad and angry but mostly confused. One thing was clear, though—she never wanted to see them again, and she'd never tell them why!

Yoshi followed Tori to the garden. He sat on her lap for a while, watching the fish. Then he threw some pebbles into the water. But there was no shade by the pond. Tori wondered how a September day in Berkeley could be this hot. An uncomfortably warm wind blew through the garden. Worse yet, dust kept getting into her eyes. As if that wasn't bad enough, someone must be burning leaves nearby. Tori took Yoshi back inside.

They played with blocks for a while, building towers Yoshi gleefully knocked down—anything to keep him away from Mama's special things, especially the row of old photographs on the living room shelf. Lined up side-by-side were framed pictures of Tori's grandparents dressed in long, dark kimonos. She liked looking at them, wondering about the ones who had died before she was born and the ones living in Japan. Would she like them? Would they like her?

Yoshi could never stay away from the small dishes of rice or the oranges Mama kept in front of the photographs. The strings of amber-colored prayer beads hanging on one of the picture frames were another of Yoshi's favorites, especially their bright orange tassels. Sometimes when Mother wasn't looking, Tori let him play with them.

This morning Yoshi was more interested in playing hide-and-seek. Tori had just found him hiding in the front closet when Mama returned, cheeks pink, beads of perspiration on her upper lip. All she could talk about was the fire.

"I could see the smoke from the store," Mama said, wiping her face with a white handkerchief.

While Tori removed the groceries from the cloth shopping bag, Mama told Tori everything, speaking rapidly in Japanese.

"Mr. Tamaro said the fire is in the hills, not far from the university. I wonder if it could be near the Griffins."

Tori didn't want to think about the Griffins today or any day, ever again. Yet she couldn't help listening to Mama's story. Probably a little brush fire, she thought. Nothing much to worry about. Besides, the Griffins' house sat near the bottom of the hills, and several blocks from the university. Even so, it wouldn't hurt to peek. Tori opened the door to the back steps. A strong gust of wind slammed it shut after she and Mama walked out.

Standing next to Mama, Tori should have had a good view of the hills. Not today. A huge cloud of smoke hid everything. The dark cloud was enormous, completely covering the hills above town, definitely the part of town where Polly lived. The scent of burning leaves was even more noticeable. Tori realized it must be coming from the fire, carried all this way by the wind. In the quiet she could hear the distant clang of fire engine bells and howling sirens.

She didn't want to care about Polly and her family. After all, they hadn't really cared about her for the last two years. It was all pretend.

"The fire isn't near them is it, Mama?" Tori asked before she could stop herself.

What she wanted Mama to say was, "Don't be silly." That didn't happen. Mama looked at her and finally said, "I don't know."

"But what if it is?"

Tori looked into the fish pond's dark blue water as she awaited Mama's answer. Perhaps the quiet pond and sleepy fish would calm her hammering heart.

Mama put her hands on Tori's shoulders, turning her around. She looked closely at Tori's face. Over the summer Tori had grown a few inches. Now she was as tall as Mama. Mama didn't say a word; she just stared at Tori for the longest time.

Mama rarely surprised Tori by doing something unexpected or acting on a whim. That's why what Mama said next really surprised her.

"Toriko, we are going to Spruce Street." Quickly she went back inside, Tori close behind. "Take Yoshi over to Mrs. Nishima's house and explain."

"But why, Mama?"

"Because I said so, that's why."

Tori didn't argue. Mama had already begun putting the last of the groceries into the icebox. Yoshi was fussy. Tori picked him up. He threw his arms around her, burying his face in the hollow of her neck. He smelled sweet, of talcum powder and Ivory soap.

How could Tori explain to Mama that she never wanted to see Polly and Jerry again? Mama wouldn't understand. Tori barely did. She dawdled on the way back from Mrs. Nishima's. If only she could think of some good reason for not going with Mama. Then she remembered that Polly and Jerry won't even be there. They'd be in school. She wouldn't have to see them.

They rode the streetcar in silence, which was fine with Tori. There was so much going on. She'd never seen the streets so crowded with people, cars, and trucks, all going in different directions. Wailing sirens, honking horns, and clanging bells came from everywhere.

Forced to a crawl, the streetcar turned into a hot, stuffy metal box. Tori's sweaty legs and back stuck to the wicker seat. The farther they traveled up University Avenue, the more people she watched filling the sidewalk. All of them looked in the same direction— toward the hills and billowing clouds of black smoke.

Policemen stood on the corners directing traffic, their cheeks puffed out from blowing their whistles, white-gloved hands frantically waving this way and that.

When the streetcar finally slowed to a stop at the corner of Spruce and Cedar, Tori jumped from her seat. Waiting impatiently for her turn to climb down the wooden steps, she peeked through a window. Nothing looked quite right. The smoke-filled sky made the neighborhood look as dark as night. When she finally stepped onto the dirt road, bits of ashes and soot flew at her face.

The short walk up Spruce Street didn't seem quite right, either. That nice feeling of being part of something special here had disappeared. Today she felt like an intruder, an outsider, someone who didn't really belong.

The Griffins were just being nice to her, their maid's poor little girl. Polly and Jerry were being kind, Mrs. Griffin polite. Agnes had been right. Tori was better off in her own neighborhood. Besides, now she knew what had upset her more than anything; all that hate hiding behind the laws. Why would people write such laws unless they hated us?

As she and Mama walked toward the Griffins' house, a powerful wind pushed against them, trying to keep them out. Tori looked at Mama.

"Mama, why did you want me to come? Why couldn't I stay at home?"

"Why, Toriko, I thought you would want to be here. I am surprised at you."

"Yes, Mama," Tori said as she looked down at the sidewalk.

Mama lowered her voice to nearly a whisper. "I thought you could help me. My English is still not good enough."

"Good enough for what?"

"I don't know." Then after a brief pause, Mama added, "What if I needed to say something to the policeman about where I was going? There were so many on the street today, weren't there?"

"Yes, Mama."

Nearing the house, Tori saw Mrs. Griffin talking with some people. Jerry and Polly were sitting on the porch steps. Tori lowered her eyes.

The Bamboo Garden

Polly spotted them right away, hopped down the steps, and ran to them, Jerry following.

"Hi! Watcha doin' here?" Polly skidded to a stop next to Tori. She didn't wait for an answer. "How're you feeling? No school today? I was supposed to go to the dentist, but Mother decided we shouldn't because of the fire. They shut our school, too! That's why Jerry's here," she finished breathlessly, throwing an arm over Jerry's shoulder.

A strange paralysis came over Tori. Her face wouldn't smile. She couldn't speak.

"Oh Tori, isn't this keen?" Polly asked. Now she grabbed Tori's hand, pulling her toward the crowd of women. "I mean, the fire up there in the hills and above campus, too! Why, I've never seen anything like this!"

"Mrs. Takahashi," Mrs. Griffin exclaimed, stopping midsentence, "I didn't expect you today on your day off. Tori, dear. How nice to see you. I hope you're feeling better."

Tori became aware of the other women standing nearby, their stares, and thin lipped mouths. She wondered if Mama had noticed.

"Yes, ma'am, I feel much better today, thank-you," she managed to get out.

"She is much better, Mrs. Griffin," Mama said

quietly. "But I wanted her to stay home from school today, to make sure."

Mama's voice was so soft that even Tori had difficulty hearing.

"I hope you don't mind our coming today. I am unable to work tomorrow, so I thought I should come today. I hope that is all right."

Tori was shocked. Mama never told stories and this was a whopper. Why would she make up such a story? A small prickle of fear raced through Tori. Could this fire be more dangerous than she imagined?

"Oh, of course, Mrs. Takahashi! What a good idea," Mrs. Griffin said. "There's still plenty to clean up from the party."

"Tori, did you know about the fire?" Polly asked excitedly.

"We could see the smoke from our house," Tori said, avoiding Polly's eyes. Then, without thinking she added, "The streetcar had trouble getting through all the police and trucks and things."

Tori realized that some of the neighbors had inched closer to their little group. Before last Saturday Tori probably wouldn't have thought much about them, especially what they thought of her. Now she couldn't keep that thought out. Were they all like Mrs. Wetherby and her nasty daughter? Do they hate us, too? Were these some of the people who made those terrible laws?

"Tori dear, what do you mean you had trouble getting through?" Mrs. Griffin asked.

"Yes, ma'am, there was lots of traffic coming down the hills. I heard one of the firemen shout something about running out of water near Buena Vista."

The other women began asking questions all at the same time.

"Did you hear which hills?"

"Did you hear more about where?"

"Did they . . ."

Questions were flying, far too many for Tori to answer. Unexpected tears made everything blurry.

"Let's go inside and get started," Mrs. Griffin interrupted, brushing a loose curl from her forehead. "If you'll excuse us, ladies."

Making a smart about-face, she walked rapidly up the walkway and into the house. Tori followed Mama, Polly, and Jerry.

The heavy front door closed behind them. Tori let herself enjoy the cool, quiet of the Griffin home — away from the smoke, the unsettling sounds of sirens and bells, and all the noisy neighbors.

By the time she walked into the living room, Polly was already stretched out on the colorful Oriental rug, head resting on the palms of her hands, legs swinging wildly in the air.

"Come on, Tori, sit here on the couch, and tell us everything," Polly said. "Did they really say there was a fire near Buena Vista? What did you see?"

Tori knew Polly's Aunt Charlotte and Uncle Horace lived on Buena Vista, high up in the Berkeley hills. Sometimes she had hiked there with Jerry and Polly. They'd arrive from their walk out of breath and hungry. Aunt Charlotte usually had something good for them to eat. Tori had never been in a house quite like theirs. "Almost like one designed by Bernard Maybeck, one of Berkeley's finest architects," Aunt Charlotte would say frequently, usually followed by, "and maybe someday he'll create a house for us!" The walls were covered with wood panels that had been left unpainted. Wood cabinets were built into all sorts of places, also unpainted. Tori always felt like a visitor in an elegant cabin in the woods. Huge eucalyptus trees hid most of the neighboring houses from view.

Just about to answer one of Polly's questions, a frantic pounding on the front door interrupted her. Polly leaped up from the rug, ran to the door and threw it open. There stood Millie, face cherry-red, breathing hard.

The Bamboo Garden

"Oh, I'm so glad you're here," the girl exclaimed. "You won't believe what's happening on campus. Why, it's just like the biggest emergency you can imagine. People are running and shouting everywhere. I think the whole university could burn down."

Chapter Fourteen

✿ Polly ✿

Mother takes Millie's arm, guiding her into the living room.

"Mrs. Takahashi, please bring Millie a glass of water. Polly, take those books off that chair so Millie can sit down."

Polly is surprised how Mother can be calm when everything is so alarming. A large out-of-control fire right above them! What does this mean? Are Jerry and Tori also a little scared? One look and she knows it's possible.

Millie removes her hat and wipes her forehead with a hanky. She takes a sip of water with slightly shaking hands. Then she cools her face with the fan Mother snatches up from the piano bench.

The Bamboo Garden

"I'll tell you, Mrs. Griffin, this is a morning I'll never forget." Millie takes a few more gulps from her glass, followed by a few flutters of her fan.

"What exactly did you see, dear?" Mother asks.

"I really didn't see it, but there's a big fire above here and on campus."

Polly sits up. Did Millie say the fire's close by? How close?

"Donald sent me. He's worried about you. He couldn't come himself. He's on his fraternity's roof with the other boys."

"What in the world for?" Mother asks.

"It's the cinders. They're flying everywhere. They've got hoses, wet blankets, and burlap bags up there. Those cinders might start a fire. He asked me to tell you what's happening."

A few more gulps of water, then Millie continues. "The wind is making things worse. Much worse! It keeps pushing the fire down the hills toward us, faster and faster!"

"Oh, Millie, Donald needn't worry. We're blocks away from all that, but how sweet of him to think of us."

Even though Mother sounds calm, that little quiver in her voice tells Polly she isn't.

"Polls, call Aunt Charlotte. I'm sure she's fine but, well, you never know." Then she turns to Millie with a reassuring smile. "Now, dear, tell me more."

Polly doesn't want to leave. She'd much rather hear Millie's story, but this is not the time to argue. The slim candlestick-shaped phone sits quietly on the hallway table. She lifts the hearing piece from the hook. Clutching its skinny neck in one hand, she dials AS for Ashberry, and then 2847. But each time she finishes, all she can hear is a busy signal. She dials so many times her finger starts to ache. But it's always the same—busy. She puts the black hearing piece back on the hook.

"Drat, everyone must be trying to get on the telephone at once," Polly mumbles to herself, just as Jerry and Tori join her in the hallway. Although annoyed, she is mostly worried. Aunt Charlotte and Uncle Horace's house is near where Millie described.

"Hey, Polly, you don't think this fire could reach here, do you?" Jerry asks, his usual smile replaced by a worried frown.

"Naw, those firemen'll put it out in no time. You saw all those engines going up the hill."

She looks at Tori, but she turns away. Gosh, she's still mad, thinks Polly. If only I could tell her about the loophole. That would make everything better.

The Bamboo Garden

Back in the living room, Millie is telling Mother and Mrs. Takahashi about her morning.

"I was sitting in my English class around eleven o'clock. My seat's right next to the window. I could see lots of black smoke coming from Founder's Rock, up in the hills just above campus. Cinders and burning grass flew right through the open windows, onto our notebooks. Golly, was it ever difficult to concentrate on Professor Haskin's Shakespeare lecture. About halfway through the class I could see all the boys who'd been in military drill that morning running by our window in their uniforms. A minute later someone came down the hallway, banging on all the doors shouting something about a fire."

As Polly listens she can't help imagining she is in a scary moving picture. She looks around the room, pretending to be the camera. Everyone else is an actor. Mother, seated across from Millie in the matching chair by the fireplace, seems calm. Polly isn't fooled. Mother's nervous habit of twirling her wedding rings gives her away. Everyone else is settled on the long red horsehair couch, opposite the piano. Mrs. Takahashi and Tori look alike, sitting stiffly, hands resting in their laps. Jerry is leaning forward, arms propped on his knees, cap dangling from one hand.

From her place on the piano bench, Polly also

has a good view of Spruce Street. Several more fire trucks speed by while Millie tells her story, their sounds muffled by the sturdy house. Millie pauses for another sip of water.

Polly jumps in. "Mother, I couldn't get through to Aunt Charlotte. All the lines are busy."

"We'll try again in a few minutes, dear." The space between Mother's eyebrows is now pinched with worry.

"So," continues Millie, refreshed by the water and clearly pleased at being the center of attention, "Professor Haskin wouldn't let us go until he finished his lecture. He's such a flat tire. His lectures always put us to sleep. We couldn't wait to leave. When we finally got out, it seemed like every boy on campus was running somewhere carrying pieces of old carpet and wet sacking. Did you hear the Campanile? That's how everyone knew something was up."

"Bernard's going to be frantic when he hears about this," Mother says to no one in particular. She twirls her rings, round and round. "Oh, that book of his. I wish San Francisco weren't so far away. He'd know what to do."

"That's why Donald wanted me to come here, ma'am. He remembered Professor Griffin was in the city. But, here's the thing. Even though plenty of students are helping to move professors' books and papers from their homes, Donald's worried they won't get to you in time. The fire may be moving too fast for that."

"Wouldn't that be great, Mother, if they could come and help?" Polly interrupts excitedly. She pictures Father's students bursting through the front door, eager to save his lifetime of work from a monstrous fire.

"Polly, now stop that. The fire is not coming here. There's no need to be so dramatic."

"But, Mrs. Griffin," Millie says. "Donald seemed sure it could."

"Well, Millie, you've certainly given us lots to think about." Mother stands up. "But really, if things are that bad, I'm sure we'll be informed by the authorities."

"I guess so." Millie's eyes sparkle with excitement. "Oh golly, this is exciting! Well, I've got to go. The girls are meeting at the student union. We're trying to get organized. I said I'd help make sandwiches for the boys fighting the fire, and I don't know what else. Maybe take care of lost children, if it comes to that."

"Yes, please run along, Millie. I'm grateful you came. Donald concerns me, though. I hope he's careful, that he doesn't do anything foolish. He loves that fraternity of his, but it's only a building."

Standing on the front porch, Polly is surprised by how fast her neighborhood changed. Only two o'clock in the afternoon, but the sky makes it seem later. Inky black, it sprinkles everything with bits of burning debris and ashes.

"Oh, I know I shouldn't say this," confides Millie, "but, gee whiz, isn't this just the bee's knees? This is soooo much better than sitting in Professor Haskin's class. Well, got to scram. Tootle-loo!"

Polly climbs onto the porch railing, wrapping her legs around its posts. She glances sideways at Tori. Is now the time? She mumbles, "I'm glad you're feeling better, Tori."

Tori doesn't answer. Polly goes on. "The party turned out swell. Aunt Charlotte came just after you left, thank goodness! Even Agnes wouldn't have had anything bad to say. Hey, speaking of Agnes, don't you think she's is full of baloney?"

Jerry and Tori are quiet. The silence makes Polly uncomfortable.

Finally, almost whispering, Tori says, "I don't want to talk about Agnes."

"Sure," Polly says.

Talking with Tori had always been easy, right from the start. Not like with other kids. Confused and hurt, Polly knows something has changed between them.

Luckily, Jerry breaks the silence.

"This whole thing is nuts! That policeman says it's just a grass fire. But, Tori, you heard about trouble on Buena Vista. We know there's a lot more than just grass up there. What about all those trees and houses?"

"You're right," Polly agrees. "And why is Donald so worried about us?"

"We've just got to find out what's going on," Jerry says, jumping down from the railing.

Polly knows he's right. But so far the police haven't been much help. Telephones aren't working. What else can they do? That's when it hits her!

"I know! I think I know how!" exclaims Polly, excited about her idea but amazed Jerry didn't think of it first.

"How?" Jerry asks.

"I know this sounds crazy, but what about your crystal set? I mean, Jerry, didn't you tell us that you'd be able to hear lots of things besides music? Didn't you say that you could hear things like news and people talking?"

"Sure, Polly. But I haven't tried it out yet. Professor Cole helped me last night. But we didn't finish. I thought I'd start it up after school today."

"Well, what're we waiting for?" Polly asks, hugely relieved to be doing something at last. "Let's go!"

Jerry takes off. Polly is about to follow but sees Tori hesitate. Without thinking, Polly grabs her hand. Tori resists at first but finally moves.

By the time they reach the Bermans' kitchen, Jerry is already sitting at the table in front of the radio. Polly never really took a good look at it before. What she sees now doesn't make any sense. Attached to a large oak plank are an assortment of wires and copper coils. Something that looks like a piece of glass about the size of an almond sits in the middle of it all.

"What's this?" Polly asks, pointing to the glass.

"The crystal," Jerry says without looking up. "That's what makes the whole thing work."

"I don't get it, Jerry. Why do they call these things a wireless? All I see are lots of wires."

Jerry doesn't seem to hear. "See, all that's left is checking out the headphone plugs."

Polly watches Jerry fiddle with the strange-looking wires. Donald sure picked the right nickname for him—the mad scientist!

"Gee, I'm almost afraid to try it! I've been at this for so long," he mumbles. He stops his fiddling and looks up, a set of earphones dangling from his hand. "What if it doesn't work?"

"Oh, come on, Jerry. It'll work. It's just got to," Polly says. "Didn't you say we'd be able to hear ships out at sea?"

"Yeah, it's terrific," he says. "With a really strong radio, we can even hear something from the other side of the world!"

Glad to see his old enthusiasm returning, she goes on. "Well then, I'm just sure we can hear someone talking about the fire from right here in Berkeley!"

Jerry shows them how to put on the earphones. Polly feels silly with these big black things on her ears. They're tight but don't hurt a bit. Slowly Jerry moves one of the wires with a sharp point until it lightly touches the crystal. What would they hear? She can't wait another second. But there is only silence. Then more silence. Jerry looks as if he might cry. Tori looks equally upset, but something tells Polly it isn't about the crystal set. There is something else on Tori's mind. Maybe this is the time to find out, and maybe she can finally tell her about the loophole. Gently she taps Tori's foot under the table.

"What?" Tori whispers crossly, not even looking at Polly.

"Oh, nothing."

She taps her foot again and then says, "This is going to work, don't you think? It's just got to!"

"No, Polly," Tori whispers back, "I don't think it's going to work. This is just another one of your dumb ideas."

"Dumb idea!"

"That's right. Dumb idea!"

"What do you mean?"

"You know what I mean!" Tori is no longer whispering.

"Hey, you two! Quiet!" Jerry shouts. "I can't hear a thing!"

Polly clamps her mouth shut. Whatever is wrong with Tori is making her nasty, so nasty Polly doesn't know what to think. She stares extra hard at Jerry and his crystal set.

"I'll try to move this antenna slider along the tuning coil. That should help us pick something up," he says, mostly to himself.

Still nothing. More silence.

Polly begins to think Tori is right, that maybe this really is a dumb idea. But then a funny noise comes through her earphones, something like a stick being dragged across a picket fence. She knows the others hear it, too.

"I'm getting something!" Jerry shouts. "I'll move this just a little bit more to the left and . . . "

That's when Polly hears the first faint but true sound of a man's voice. Jerry fiddles a little more. He moves one of his wires a tiny bit. Polly hears something that makes her jump. The man's voice is now so clear it's as if he's standing in the next room.

"Yep, folks, this is one *co-lo-ssal* fire! We understand

the fire department's trying to decide whether to ask for help from nearby towns. San Francisco, Oakland, Emeryville, Piedmont, and Richmond have all been mentioned. However, we've also learned that Oakland is fighting several small fires themselves. Residents are urged to stay away from the fire area, especially above Buena Vista. The fire's moving fast. There's a real possibility the whole town could be reduced to ashes in a matter of hours."

Chapter Fifteen

⚘ Polly ⚘

Wide-eyed, Polly looks at Tori and Jerry. Did they hear what the man said? They did. She can see it in their eyes. The fire is near, close to Aunt Charlotte's house. Even worse, it is racing toward them! No one moves until Polly takes off her earphones.

"Let's tell your mom," Jerry says in a whisper.

Polly heads for the door and down the stairs; Tori's and Jerry's footsteps close behind.

"Be back in a minute," Jerry yells when they reach Polly's back steps.

Polly watches him sprint toward the driveway, then hurries into the house. Mother and Mrs. Takahashi are at the credenza, putting away silver trays from the party.

"Mother! Mother! Millie and Donald are right. The fire's coming this way! We've got to leave!"

"Please, Polly, slow down. I can't understand you!"

"The fire's coming, Mrs. Griffin," Tori says, "We heard all about it on Jerry's wireless."

"The man says a fire's coming and really fast! He says it could burn up the whole city. It's heading for us now!"

Jerry runs into the dining room shouting. "Come on! You've got to see this!"

Polly is the first one to the front porch. Spruce Street has completely changed. The road is clogged with cars, all heading down hill and most stuffed so full she can hardly see the passengers.

Dust from the road traffic mingles with the ash. Thick black smoke blocks all sunlight. Polly brushes the porch railing, now covered with white and gray ash—more than enough to write her name in.

"Oh, dear," Mother says, hands raised to her cheeks. "What shall we do?"

The view from the porch shocks Polly. Lots of people are walking, many with strange, empty looks on their faces. Some of them look creepy, especially the ones holding onto the most peculiar things. One lady has a feather duster and another an umbrella even though it hasn't rained for months and none in sight.

The parade of people and cars keeps a steady pace. Polly wonders how they can just walk away from their homes. She'd never do that! She'd think of something to do, something to save her house from the fire. Donald and his fraternity brothers didn't run away. Visions of the boys on the roof give her an idea.

"Mother, why don't we get a hose up on the roof like Donald did? We can do it. I know how to get up there."

Polly imagines standing next to the chimney, hose in hand. She'd spray the roof's wooden shingles, bravely putting out any flames daring to get near. Wait! What is she thinking? Not the roof! She hates heights.

"Polly, just put that crazy idea out of your mind. I don't want you children up there. Do you hear me?" Mother stops her pacing long enough to look into Polly's eyes.

"Yes, Mother," Polly says, relieved.

"We're leaving!" Mother says with a shaky voice. Then more determinedly, "Yes. That's it. We must. Right now! A few things in the car and we go. Quickly now, we haven't much time."

"I'll get a few things from my bedroom," Polly offers, eager to be helpful.

"No, Polls. Books, we need to save Father's books

and papers. Oh, dear, I'm not even sure I know what to take."

Polly watches her mother in alarm. She's never seen her really frightened.

"Polly. You help Mrs. Takahashi put some silver into the automobile. You know—platters, candlesticks, punch bowl. I'll go to Father's study. Jerry, Tori, come with me. You can help take things outside. Hurry now!"

Mrs. Takahashi hands Polly a few silver trays and the candleholders. Polly stuffs them into the automobile and hurries back. She sees Tori and Jerry racing back and forth from the study. A few more trips and the silver drawer is empty.

"I'll just take a look around upstairs now, Mother," Polly says.

She dashes up the steps, two at a time, and then hurries into her bedroom. Nothing feels real. How could this be happening? Her brand-new straw hat is on the bed. Placing it on her head, she looks around. What else can she take? Her skates, of course, and what about the bag of marbles on the toy shelf? The licorice rope she and Jerry bought for Tori on Saturday seems important. Skates in one hand, marbles in the other, and licorice in her pocket, Polly looks around the room one more time. "Don't burn," she begs silently as she looks at her four-poster bed. "Don't burn," she says softly as she looks around at all the things she loves—the toys and dolls sitting quietly on her shelf; the collection of assorted rocks and twigs she brought home, certain they were once used by Indians; yesterday's arrowhead; and the kite Tori and Jerry helped her make that time she was sick in bed with the mumps.

Jerry and Tori are waiting on the front porch.

"Gotta go now," Jerry says. "Maybe get some of our things together in case Mom gets home. You'll be OK, right?"

"Yeah, sure. We're just fine," Polly says, not believing a word.

"Great. Now get going."

Jerry wipes his wet forehead with the back of his arm then pulls his white handkerchief from his pants. Something falls to the floor. He picks it up.

"Why, looky here!"

He holds up the wooden nickel. Polly forgot all about it.

He hands it to Tori. "I think it's your turn to make a wish," he says. Polly watches her hesitate before reaching out a hand.

"But you've only had it a few days," Tori protests.

"Yeah, but you hold onto it now. After all this excitement is over you can give it back. I sure don't want to lose it. Anyhow, my wish can wait. Well, see you."

Jerry jogs down the steps and heads to his apartment. Guiltily, Polly wonders why she didn't think of him sooner. His mother's at work. What'll he do? Her worries about Jerry vanish when a strong gust of wind picks up her new hat, carrying it down the street. She watches until it disappears. Hat gone, Polly can't shake the feeling that something else is missing.

Tori calls to her.

"Polly!" Tori is next to the automobile. Father's books are sitting on the ground in a tall pile. "Can't fit these in," she says.

Polly shoves several of them into tiny spaces here and there, Tori helping alongside. As Polly pushes the last one behind the back seat, Tori suddenly freezes. Polly glances at her. One hand holds onto a book and the other is curled into a fist. What did I do now, Polly wonders. Is Tori going to punch me?

Polly hears a familiar voice behind them.

"You two are certainly busy little bees."

Polly looks over her shoulder.

"Oh, Agnes, you scared me!" Polly climbs out from the back seat. Agnes is wearing a white dress with red trim—and a nasty smirk.

"You shouldn't creep up on people like that."

"I'm just standing here. It's a free country, you know."

Then, more quietly, as if sharing a secret for Polly's ears only, "I'd watch my things if I were you, Polly Griffin. You can never tell what *they* will do when you're not looking."

The last time Agnes said mean things, Polly was so shocked she could barely speak. This time, she's ready.

"Agnes, go home. Tori and I aren't interested. In fact, we're not interested in anything you have to say, ever again." She glares at Agnes, making her face look as angry as she feels. "Tori can do anything she wants. We don't need you around telling us what we can and can't do."

Agnes doesn't seem to hear. She goes on.

"Well, we're putting *our* possessions on the porch. Father and some of his reliable workmen will be coming to take them away."

All she sees of Agnes is her cruel smile. Rage growing, Polly wants to hurl herself at this awful girl, hurt her, make her sorry for saying mean things. Clenching both hands tightly, Polly stares fiercely at her target—Agnes's ugly nose. Mother's voice interrupts.

"Hello, Agnes. Did you come over to help? How kind of you."

Agnes turns slowly toward Mrs. Griffin. In a syrupy sweet voice, she says, "I'm sorry I'm too late to help, Mrs. Griffin. Polly tells me you're already finished packing up your car."

"Thank-you, Agnes. I think we can manage. You'd better go home now and help your mother."

Agnes flashes Mother an angelic smile. "Yes, ma'am. That's a good idea."

What a phony, thinks Polly. *When I'm done with her, she'll never smile again.* Mother's firm grip on Polly's shoulder distracts her—all pretense of calm evaporated.

"Girls, help me! The automobile key! I can't find it. I've looked everywhere."

If there were ever a time Polly wanted to tell her mother about mean and spiteful Agnes, this is it! But she can't. Mother is a mess. Red splotches on her face seem to be working their way down her neck. The hot wind blows blond curls into her eyes, which she keeps trying to brush away. Anyway, such talk would only embarrass Mrs. Takahashi, who is now standing by the car.

"I usually leave it in the ignition. But now I can't find it anywhere. I don't know what I'll do if we can't move this thing!"

"Did you look in the laundry room, on the wall hook?" Polly asks.

"The hook, why yes, of course. That's where it is. I forgot. Polly, run inside and get it. Hurry."

When Polly runs through the house, she gets the most peculiar feeling. Something isn't right. But what? Is it Tori? Probably. They never fought before. Now everything is upside down. Polly is back quickly, key in hand. Mrs. Takahashi and Tori are already squeezed into the front seat leaving a little space for her.

"Oh, Polly, you found it. Get in, quickly! I'm sure I saw flames just now, up the hill there."

"Where we going, Mother?"

"Father's office. We'll be safe on campus. We can let Tori and her mother off downtown."

Before Polly can squeeze in, Mother puts the key in the switch and turns. Polly holds her breath. Father fixed their Model T so Mother didn't need to use the hand crank. Although the switch is supposed to make driving easier, Polly hasn't seen her use it yet. Mother turns the key a second time. Nothing. Biting her lower lip, Mother tries again. This time the engine kicks on.

"Oh, thank goodness," Mother murmurs, releasing the long hand brake poking up from the floor. At the same time, she presses the brake pedal down. On the steering wheel, she pushes the spark lever up, the gas lever down. The car jerks forward.

"Scoot over, everyone," she yells. "I need more room."

Polly leans forward to see Mother work the three floor pedals. This is the tricky part. Can she get the automobile to go without stalling? The leg pushing down on the brake pedal trembles. Polly crosses her fingers on both hands. *Come on, Mother; you've got to do it!* They inch out to the road.

"Now, if only those drivers let me in," Mother frets.

Polly doesn't think it's possible. Automobiles jam the street, and Mother is so tiny. Will anyone even see her in the driver's seat? Mother keeps talking as she waits for an opening in the line of cars.

"It looks like everyone's coming down the hill now! Why, there goes Professor Loftly's wife! Oh my, aren't those the Doughertys?"

Mother recognizes at least three other families. Most of the drivers are women, children squeezed in next to them. What amazes Polly most are the things loaded into the automobiles, especially the rumble seats in the back. Wedged in are lamps, sewing machines, even fur coats. One car drives by with a black-and-white milk cow tied to the back fender. Her moos are pitiful.

Did Mother make the right choices? Did Polly? Tori's knee accidentally bumps hers. Before the fight, Polly couldn't wait to tell Tori about the loophole that would surely change their lives. But there wasn't a chance. Does it matter anymore? There was that fight, and then Agnes came along, making everything worse.

When Mother gets onto the street at last, the heavy traffic makes for slow going. As automobiles stream down from the hills, all sorts of trucks are heading up loaded with men, shovels, hoses, and stacks of burlap bags.

Finally arriving downtown, Polly watches the huge crowds of people jamming the sidewalk. It's like she's in a parade. No one is looking at them, though. They are pointing up toward the hills. She turns around. So does Tori. With the car roof down, there is a clear view.

"Oh, Mother! We can see the fire. We can see where it is!" Mother, hands clenching the huge steering wheel, does not look. There are stalled cars everywhere, horns honking, and lots of shouting.

"Everything is black above the fire. There are lots of flames and black smoke. It's huge!"

Even though Polly is relieved they got away, fear creeps through her. But like a moth attracted to light, she can't help looking back one more time. A huge wall of flame races down the hill. The fierce wind fans and flattens the fire, which is now leaping from one brown-shingled home to the next. Every now and then fire turns a tree into a giant torch. Is her imagination playing tricks on her? Did that house just explode into a fiery ball? One look at Tori's face tells her it did.

Without warning, Mother honks the horn, then jams her foot onto the brake pedal, slamming everyone into the dashboard. The engine is silent. They've stalled.

"Oh dear! I've never seen anything like this," Mother says. "Tori, you and your mother better get out here. I'm sure you'll be able to catch a streetcar nearby."

"We will, Mrs. Griffin," Tori says. "Come on, Mama."

Polly slides off the front seat and stands on the running board so Tori and her mother can scoot out. Mrs. Takahashi hesitates for a second. That's when Polly remembers the licorice rope stuffed into her dress pocket.

"Hey Tori, this is for you. It's from Saturday. I'm sure it's still good," she says, releasing the sticky candy from her grasp.

As Tori takes the black candy, her eyes meet Polly's. "Thanks."

"That's OK."

Tori holds her mother's hand to steady her as she climbs down from the car's wide running board. Polly watches Tori and Mrs. Takahashi make their way through the crowded sidewalk, still holding hands.

Several red and glowing cinders land on the automobile's black hood. They are blown off as the car finally lurches forward, replaced by a handful of gray ashes. The fire is getting closer.

Chapter Sixteen

ॐ Polly ॐ

Slowly, they move along the crowded, chaotic street. Clutching the edge of the seat, Polly bumps up and down alongside Mother.

Everyone knows Mother is the better driver in the family. Still, all this confusion and noise don't help. To make matters worse, the Model T is too big for her. For ages, Polly listened to Mother pester Father about buying one of those newer, smaller touring cars. Now, sitting on two extra cushions, she can barely see over the dashboard and steering wheel. But with a sigh of relief, Mother finally makes the turn onto campus.

Big black automobiles are parked everywhere, most loaded down like theirs. Male students are sprawled against trees or on the grass, faces black from smoke and soot. Huge piles of furniture, typewriters, suitcases, and other odds and ends are scattered everywhere.

"I guess we aren't the only ones with this idea, Mother."

"Guess so, Polls," Mother says, coasting to a stop near Father's building, then struggling to pull up the long hand brake. "Uhhh! There now, that should do it!"

The moment Polly jumps from the car's running board, a huge explosion shakes the ground.

"Mother, that's another house exploding, just like the one I saw from the car. The fire touched it and *bang*—it turned into a fire-ball!"

Nearby a tall, thin woman clutches the hands of two rosy-cheeked little girls.

"Oh, no, my dear," the woman interrupts. "You've got that wrong. It's dynamite."

"Dynamite! Why in the world would anyone use dynamite in the midst of all of this?" Mother asks reaching for Polly, arms encircling her, hugging her close. Polly is still, afraid to move, wanting Mother's arms there forever.

"To make a fire-break, dear."

"What do you mean?"

"They think if they dynamite homes, then there

won't be any place for the fire to go. It will burn out. Or so they hope."

"Why, that doesn't make any sense."

"I quite agree. It's like they're adding kindling to the flames. They wanted to blow up our house. I don't know if they did. They made us leave. We're up on Euclid."

"Euclid! You mean the fire reached there?" Mother hugs Polly tighter.

"Indeed. You can't imagine what we saw. We had only seconds to leave. Thank goodness, some students came to help. We could see the fire. The heat was incredible."

The lady is so desperate to talk that she seems about to explode. "Those students were wonderful," she goes on, hardly stopping to breathe. "Some of them carried old Mr. Bridges out of his house. He's been confined to his bed for a while, far too sick and weak to walk down the stairs. I was so worried about him."

Another explosion shakes the ground. Polly freezes. As soon as things are quiet again, the lady goes on.

"They're thinking about dynamiting some of the houses farther down the hill. They mentioned Spruce Street. I sure hope they know what they're doing."

"Spruce Street! Why that's where we live. You can't mean it!" Mother's arms hug Polly tighter.

"Well, that's what I heard."

One of the little girls is tugging on her mother's hand.

"Please excuse me. I promised the girls we'd get something to drink at the student union."

Dynamite? Spruce Street? Her beautiful house? Mother unwraps her arms from Polly's shoulders.

"Polly, let's go."

"Where?"

"We're going back to the house."

"Why?"

"Because no one is going to dynamite anything, if I have my say."

Polly runs after Mother across the dry, sunburned fields in the direction of their house. Quickly they reach the edge of campus. Police and fire trucks are everywhere, blocking the way.

"S'cuse me, ma'am!" shouts one of the policemen when Mother starts to walk over the web of hoses lying in the street, Polly close behind. "I'd stop there. You really don't want to go any farther than this. It's not safe."

Mother steps back, pulling Polly with her. Standing there side by side, holding hands, Polly is hypnotized by the dreadful sight before them.

Flames are leaping from house to house, pouring

out of windows and doors. After a few minutes, the house collapses. A few crumple with surprising speed, some in slow motion. The fire is now a gigantic, smelly monster, crushing everything in its way.

"Ouch!" Polly shakes her head. Something stings her and it isn't a bee. A shower of glowing red cinders falls from the black cloud of smoke overhead. One must have landed on her hair, burning her scalp.

"Move back, move back!" the policeman shouts to the crowd of bystanders, all spellbound by the sight of flying cinders.

An automobile jammed full of students races by, some still wearing their blue-and-khaki football uniforms from morning practice.

"Look out, everyone! We're going to dynamite!" they shout.

"Mother!" Polly yells, pointing to a bunch of students standing on a roof.

Long watering hoses snake up the sides of the building. The boys are hosing down wooden shingles. Some are setting out wet blankets and burlap bags. Others are dragging or carrying furniture out of the building.

Two firemen, their faces already blackened by smoke, are deep in conversation. Their voices are loud enough for Polly to hear everything through the noise.

"Those Spruce houses are gonna hafta go."

"I think you're right. Could make the perfect fire break," agrees the second.

"If the fire gets any farther, there's no tellin' how fast it'll travel. With this wind, the fire could reach downtown in no time."

"Yeah, but still, there's no tellin' if dynamite'll do the trick. Water isn't working! Chemical trucks are empty. That wind just keeps fanning the flames. Let's call the men together. We've got to decide, and fast."

Mother lets go of Polly's hand and briskly approaches the firemen.

"You're not going to do anything of the kind!" she shouts, looking up into the men's faces with an expression Polly knows only too well.

When Mother looks like that, Father would raise his bushy eyebrows extra high, give a little cough, then fall silent. He knows better than to disagree.

"Now you two listen here . . . , " she says, balancing on tiptoe so that her finger could jab the jacket of the man with the most brass buttons.

Polly doesn't hear the rest of Mother's sentence or any of the many sounds surrounding them. She is watching a shaggy brown dog running away from the fire, ears flattened against his head, tail between his legs. The sight of the frightened dog jolts Polly clear through. *Fudge!* She forgot all about Fudge! How is that possible?

Images of her flop-eared bunny flash before her—Fudge, sleeping under the kitchen table cuddled up in a soft pink blanket. With the excitement of the fire and all, the bunny simply vanished from her mind. Oh, that seems like ages ago. Was it only this morning Fudge finally ate a little, even acted peppier?

Frightening images of Fudge alone in the house make everything around her fade away. *The fire! The noise! Poor little Fudge. She must be scared to death! How could I have forgotten her? I've got to get her! That's what I should do. The fire couldn't be at Spruce Street yet. Mother won't know. I'll just dash over there, grab Fudge, and be back before Mother even knows I'm gone. It's only six or seven blocks.*

Carefully, she backs away—one step, then another, and another. Mother doesn't notice. All her attention is directed at jabbing the brass buttons of the second, shorter fireman, tiptoes no longer needed.

Polly takes off at a run. Home and Fudge are only minutes away. She imagines holding the bunny in her arms on her return to campus. But just as she reaches Spruce Street, a policeman steps in front of her.

"Hey, young lady! Whatcha doin? Wrong way!"

Polly looks up at a sweaty, red-faced man, his black

wool uniform unbuttoned at the neck. Perspiration drips from his nose and chin. Right away she knows he'd never understand what she must do.

"Yes, sir," she says, backing up a few steps.

Satisfied, the policeman quickly turns his attention back to directing traffic. Until this moment, Polly's only thoughts are about rescuing Fudge. Now she can see it won't be easy. People will try to stop her. How is she going to sneak past everyone?

Being invisible would help. That's when she remembers the gray mouse living in her sleeping porch — the one who watched Polly from under the desk. At just the right moment, when Polly wasn't looking, he'd scurry around looking for leftover crumbs. Whiskers twitching, he'd keep one eye on Polly, always ready to hide. That's what she'd do — make herself as small, sneaky, and brave as that little mouse.

A row of cars parked along the street will be a good place to start. All she has to do is let the automobiles hide her. Darting from auto to auto is easy. The noise, confusion, and thick smoke helps.

Unfortunately, she soon runs out of cars. But by now most of the commotion is far away. The only people around are so busy hosing down their homes they don't notice her. The Spruce Street traffic

Mother steered through earlier is down to a trickle. No homes burning, either.

The farther Polly runs, the darker it gets, so dark she is startled when someone grabs her arm with such force she nearly falls down.

"Hey, little girl, you're going the wrong way!"

A young man wearing a blue-and-gold beanie is tugging at her.

"Come on with me. Hurry!"

A student! His cap gives him away — the freshman beanie.

"Let go! I'm fine!"

"No, you're not! The fire is just behind me. Come on!"

"No!"

Black soot and ashes smudge his face and white shirt. Big and burly, he seems more likely to throw her over his shoulder than argue.

"Let go, I said!" Polly screams.

She twists her arm from his grasp, the way Jerry showed her when they play-wrestled. It works. She's free. Running hard, she hopes the smoke will keep hiding her. No footsteps. Did he give up? Taking no chances, Polly decides to stay away from the road. Better to stick close to the houses with their bushes and porches. Only a few more blocks to go.

The fire has turned her beautiful neighborhood into a bad dream. But her tired legs are no dream. She forgot how Spruce Street goes uphill, not much of a hill, but now it matters. Much too tired for running, she feels like someone tied weights to her ankles. The stinky smoke swirled about by a gusty wind stings her eyes and throat.

Now and then flames shoot out a window. The few people hosing down their homes are busy. They don't notice her. Polly is invisible.

Two students, each with a young child in their arms, run her way. Will they see her? Quickly, she crouches by the side of a porch. They race by. Not even a glance in her direction. Polly hurries on. This running and hiding takes precious time.

The wind blows ash and smoke into her eyes. They sting. Her chest hurts, too. Struggling, she goes on to the next house. Just as she reaches a new porch, a blast of heat sears the back of her legs and arms. Gasping for breath, she stumbles a few steps before falling down. From here, she sees what happened. The house turned into a ball of fire. Spellbound, she watches the walls start a slow, silent collapse, crumbling like a tower of playing cards. Head throbbing, legs shaking, she makes herself get up. *Got to get away. Get to the road. I'll be safe there. I'll be safe at home. Nothing bad can happen there. Keep going. Keep going. Hurry.*

The Bamboo Garden

One block from her goal, Polly watches several more homes crumple to the ground. A shower of sparks and glowing embers is all that is left behind. Going back to Mother now seems just as dangerous as going on. Fear and exhaustion make it hard for Polly to think, but images of Fudge, alone and frightened, tug at her.

With wobbly legs, eyes stinging, flames all around, houses collapsing everywhere, Polly is terrified. A porch across the street tempts her. Covering her nose and mouth with the hem of her skirt helps make it easier to breathe. Bright orange flames claw at her, catlike. Finally at the porch, Polly collapses on the bottom step. The view is horrifying. Is that the Anderson home on fire? Fire licks at the front porch of the Wetherby place, flaming brighter as it reaches the rose-covered trellis. More flames pour from the upstairs windows toward the roof.

Oh, I'm too late. The fire—at our house! Must be! So tired. Don't think I can make it. Can't stay here. But Fudge! Got to save her. Close my eyes. Make everything go away.

Polly is out of good ideas. Maybe Tori was right after all. "Another one of your dumb ideas" was what she had said.

She peeks at the Wetherby house—now a crumbled, flaming heap of burnt wood. But what's this?

No! It's not possible! Her house! It's still there, standing all by itself. Everything about it is perfect--trees, flowers, porch swing, front steps. Is Fudge inside, waiting for her to come through the front door?

Once inside, Polly races to the kitchen. The pink blanket is still under the table. She kneels down, eager to hold the bunny in her arms. But no Fudge! Could the bunny be hiding in the soft folds of the blanket? She lifts it up. No Fudge here. No soft, furry bunny to hold, to kiss, stroke, and say, "I'm sorry, I'm sorry!"

Tears fill her eyes.

"Fudge, where are you?" Polly shouts, now frantic. "Here Fudge! I've come home! Where are you?"

The house is quiet. No sirens, explosions, horns, shouts, just a peaceful calm. Frantically she begins her search, all the while keeping watch for the silent arrival of fire. Fudge's favorite places are empty—the bedrooms, under the couch and Father's desk, and upstairs in the laundry basket. Nothing! Suddenly the house shakes. Outside are crashing sounds, and window-rattling booms. Are they dynamiting Spruce Street?

"Oh, Fudge, where are you?" she shouts, over and over.

The dull thud of another explosion vibrates the house, rattling windows and shaking the floor. Before looking under her bed one last time, Polly glances out the window that looks onto the street. The house where she rested a few minutes ago is now a flaming orange ball. Can she see dynamiters? She leans out the window for a look. Her view is blocked by the porch roof below.

But what's that on the corner of the roof? Something bright and orange. An ember! It must be. The fire has come to Polly's house. These are the embers Donald and his buddies watched out for. What did they do? Wet towels! And water!

Frantically she looks around her room for something to splash on the hot cinder. Her boxes! The yellow one's the biggest. She dumps her rock collection onto the floor and races to the bathroom sink. Turning the water on full force, she waits. Nothing—not even a drop! She runs to the other bathroom. Same thing. The fire! Must have to do with the fire.

Back in her bedroom, she checks the roof. A small plume of smoke now rises from the glowing ember, but no flames yet. Where to get water—at least enough to wet something? Fudge's water dish! There's not much in it, but it's something. Under the dish is the towel Mother makes sure she keeps there. She dumps the water onto the towel then checks out the ember. Still no flame but definitely more smoke. Can she smother the ember by tossing Fudge's wet towel on top of it? What if she misses? It's far too terrible to imagine. She has no choice. She must climb out her window and walk on the roof. She'd done this once before to show off for Jerry and Tori. It was stupid of her. Now she has to do it again.

Don't look down! Whatever you do, don't look down! She sits on the roof then scoots on her bottom to the ember, hugging the wet towel tight, closer and closer until she's an arm's length away. *Careful now, do it right. One chance. If it doesn't work, you've got to get out of the house, and fast!*

She flaps open the towel and gingerly hurls it over the glowing embers, holding onto an end.

A gratifying sizzle greets her ears — the wet towel worked! She did it! Scooting backward to the window, Polly takes one more look. Nothing! No embers, no glow, no smoke, just a wet towel lying on the edge of the little roof.

Exhausted, Polly crawls on the floor for a last peek under her bed. Nothing.

I know I should go. Can't save Fudge. Gotta save myself.

Her bed with its soft yellow-and-white blanket tempts her.

A little rest, and then I'll find Mother. Just close my eyes for a bit. Can't hurt. So tired.

Chapter Seventeen

❦ Tori ❦

Tori took a last look at Polly and Mrs. Griffin driving away in the big black car. Just the top of Polly's head was visible, not much more of Mrs. Griffin. Tori couldn't imagine how Mrs. Griffin will get that big automobile to campus safely. As they drove off, Tori saw a few loose papers fly out of the back seat. Had they come from the box of Professor Griffin's work? Then she remembered she didn't care anymore.

Mama walked briskly to the trolley stop. Blaring sirens, horns, and shouts made talking impossible, so Tori just clutched Mama's hand. When the streetcar finally arrived, Mama's face relaxed.

"You two are lucky," the conductor said as Mama dropped a few coins into the glass-and-metal box at his side. "This is the last streetcar of the day. They're not letting any more of us through."

Expertly, he flipped the little handle, letting the coins drop down into the coin box. The streetcar was practically empty.

"Yep, too dangerous for us to go up Spruce Street anymore!" the conductor shouted over his shoulder from his place on the wooden stool. "They say the fire may burn up the whole downtown!"

Neither Mama nor Tori said anything. Giving up on them, he turned his attention to an elderly woman who had just climbed aboard. Tori was glad. She wanted to put the fire out of her mind. Seeing that house explode had frightened her. It looked like a toy—nothing more than a toothpick structure lit by a match, then burnt to a crisp in seconds. What bothered her most was that she hadn't seen any flames on the house. It just blew up, all by itself.

It was only three o'clock when they arrived home, still plenty of time for Mama to start dinner. Tori's job was to keep Yoshi busy in the garden. A few minutes later, Haruo and Kenji joined them.

Haruo, nine and the older of the two, was nearly as tall as Tori. A thick handful of black hair covered his eyes, even though he plastered it down with water every morning. In his arms he carried an old rag, a can of oil, and his baseball mitt. Sometimes

Tori wondered if Haruo loved oiling that smelly mitt more than playing ball.

Kenji followed, a shorter version of Haruo except for a few missing front teeth. Tori had hoped to have some time to herself. No such luck now that the boys were there. Little brothers were so annoying.

"Mama told us you saw the fire," Haruo said.

"Tell us all about it, Tori, please," Kenji begged. "Did you see the flames?"

Kenji loved fire engines. Ever since he could talk, he'd plead with Tori to take him to the nearby firehouse. He'd stand there on the sidewalk in front of the station, holding onto Tori's hand, never showing the slightest desire to leave. The firemen didn't seem to mind those nearly daily visits. If things were quiet, they might let him stand on the running board of the hose truck. Once, they put him in the front seat. After that Tori noticed he had become even crazier about fire equipment and firemen.

"Did you see any pumpers working? Oh, I wish I'd been there."

Pumpers were his favorite. He could go on and on about them. "If it weren't for the pumpers," he'd explain to anyone listening, "only trickles of water would come out of the hose."

To Tori, the pumper looked like a giant milk can going for a ride on a wagon. She could see her reflection in the highly polished steel pipes attached to its side. Kenji liked to run his hand over the brightly painted red, gold, and black spokes of its giant wheels.

One time the stoker showed Kenji how he did his work, feeding coal into the bottom of the pumper so the water would keep boiling.

"See, Tori, if the stoker let those hot coals die, why then there wouldn't be any steam," Kenji would tell her on their walks home from the station. "So if there isn't any steam, then the pumper wouldn't have any pressure to fill those hoses with water. It's an important job."

Kenji told everyone how he wanted to be a stoker when he grew up.

"I'll bet those pumpers are working hard today. Hope they don't run out of coal. It's hard work, stoking, you know," Kenji added importantly.

He sat down on the grass, crossed his legs, and looked up at Tori expectantly. Haruo had already begun work on his mitt. Yoshi snuggled into Kenji's lap. Tori looked at the three boys. Well, she might as well take advantage of their willingness to be still for a few moments. But which part of the story should she tell?

She decided to start at the end, at the part of the

story that still made her head spin, the part where she watched the monster fire from the safety of the Griffins' car. She told them how the flames danced and leaped in the air, how the house on the hill exploded from the heat, and how lots and lots of people came down from the hills, carrying anything they could.

"Did you see anyone get burned?" Haruo asked, looking up from his mitt.

"No, Haruo, we didn't see anything like that."

How disgusting! She paused for a moment, recalling the scene with Agnes. No, she'd never tell them about that! Then that fight with Polly. That had to be the worst moment in her life. Why did she yell like that? Nothing made any sense.

"Mama and I helped Polly and Mrs. Griffin fill up their car. There wasn't an inch of room by the time we finished. Some of the cars coming down the hill were so loaded, there was hardly a place for passengers. You should have seen this one car. If it weren't such a scary time, you might think it looked kind of funny. Their rumble seat was crammed full with two huge dogs."

"I'll bet they were plenty scared," Kenji offered.

"You bet! All those sirens and excitement didn't help much," she added.

Tori grew quiet with the picture of those two

frightened dogs in her mind. Two frightened dogs? The idea made her think of something awful.

Fudge! In all the excitement, they had forgotten about Fudge! How did that happen? What were they thinking? Why didn't anyone say something like, "Who's got the bunny?" or "Wonder where Fudge went?"

Abruptly, Tori stood up. The idea of Fudge being alone in the house certain to burn down or explode frightened her. Tears filled her eyes. The stomachache that had kept her home started up again.

"Hey, Tori, what's the matter?" Kenji asked.

"Fudge! We forgot Fudge!"

The boys knew all about Fudge. Tori talked as much about Fudge as Kenji did about his pumper wagons. Yoshi, tired of Kenji's lap, started to squirm. He raised his arms to Tori. Distracted by thoughts of Fudge, she lifted him and began to nervously bounce him on her hip.

"How could you forget her?" Haruo asked, his glove no longer the center of interest.

"I don't know! It just happened."

The screen door slammed shut. It was Papa, home sooner than usual.

"How nice to see all my children together."

As if reading their thoughts he added, "We closed

the nursery early today. Mr. Carlson's home is near the fire, so he wanted to be there. There were few customers. This fire has everyone worried."

Yoshi squirmed out of Tori's arms. He tottered toward Papa.

"Papa, did Mama tell you about the Griffins?" Tori asked.

"Yes, Toriko. That was very good of you two to help out. I am proud of you."

"But Papa, something terrible happened! We forgot something important!"

"I'll say," said Haruo, a little too eagerly. "They forgot Fudge!"

"Oh, Papa, what should we do?" she asked, voice trembling.

Papa lifted Yoshi in one arm, and then reached for Tori's hand. "Come on, let's go inside."

On their way, Tori sensed a sudden change in the garden. Papa must have noticed, too. He stopped midway on the steps.

"Well, I think that terrible wind has finally calmed down. Look at the bamboo, children. Do you remember how the wind nearly flattened those stalks to the ground? I wasn't worried. Bamboo is both delicate and strong at the same time. But look now. What do you see?"

"They're still blowing, Papa," Kenji said.

"Yeah, but the other way," Haruo piped in enthusiastically.

"And the wind isn't blowing as hard, Papa," Tori added.

"You're all right, and something else. I do believe this new wind has brought us some welcome sea air—cool and damp. This is good. Maybe the fire will slow down. Now, let's go see if Mama has dinner ready."

Papa's rough, sandpapery hand calmed Tori. The sea breeze could only mean good things. By the time everyone was gathered around the dinner table, Tori's fears for Fudge had faded a bit. Maybe Polly's house hadn't burned down. Maybe the Griffins remembered Fudge, after all. Maybe at this very minute Fudge was nibbling on that extra lettuce Polly had left her just that morning.

"I brought Mr. Carlson's truck home with me," Papa said toward the end of the meal. "Morning deliveries."

Haruo pushed his chair back and raced to the front window. "Yep, there it is! Did you have trouble getting that engine started? I can help you with the crank in the morning if you want."

"Papa, can we go . . . see the fire . . . after dinner?"

The Bamboo Garden

Kenji shoveled Mama's soba noodles into his mouth with his chopsticks, talking at the same time. Everyone loved Mama's cold noodles on hot nights, especially Kenji.

"Kenji, don't talk with your mouth full," Mama said from her end of the table.

"Papa, please," he begged. "You could take us in the truck."

"Oh, yes, Papa! That's a good idea! We wouldn't have to get too close. We could drive a few blocks away, just for the view," Tori said, excited now.

What a day! She hadn't wanted to go see Polly in the first place and that terrible argument only made things worse. More than anything, she was relieved to be away from the fire. Now she couldn't wait to go back, but that was mainly because of Fudge.

"Tori said there were pumper wagons there. Maybe we could see the hook-'n-ladders and hose trucks, too. Come on, Papa, please say yes," Kenji pleaded.

Papa looked at Mama.

"I suppose it will be all right, if you do not go near the fire," she said reluctantly. "I'll stay here with Yoshi. I've had enough excitement for today. But first, everyone has to finish their *gomae*."

Without saying a word, the boys obediently cleaned their plates. Tori had never seen them eat spinach so quickly, without complaint. Tori didn't care for it, either. Still, if she didn't finish the green things, Mama might not let her go.

Tonight the truck started up with only one turn of the crank. Tori sat next to Papa on the front seat while the boys clambered into the truck bed, sitting between the potted trees waiting for delivery. Papa drove up Grove Street, then turned right on University Avenue, the same route Tori and Mama had traveled in the morning. As the sun began its descent, instead of darkness the early evening sky glowed bright red—a fire-lit sky.

"Toriko, you know we're just going to take a look, don't you?"

"Yes, Papa."

"Most of the fire is probably out by now."

"But that red sky, what do you think that means, Papa?"

"We'll see."

By the time they parked and walked a few blocks through the crowd of onlookers, Tori understood the red sky. Flames no longer jumped from house to house. There was only a hill of smoldering red-hot bricks and rubble.

"Why, there's nothing left!" Haruo exclaimed. "Nothing but piles of bricks."

"And chimneys," Kenji said, almost in a whisper.

All that remained of the elegant homes and tree-lined streets she had loved was a forest of chimneys. The Griffin home could not have escaped this fire. And Fudge! Oh dear, poor little Fudge. Although she knew it wasn't right to worry so much about a bunny, she couldn't help feeling as if her heart were splitting in two. She loved that bunny. Before this moment Tori had some vague idea she would be able to save Fudge. Now she saw it was impossible.

"Hey, look at that!" Haruo pointed to an old woman hugging a large bird cage to her chest.

"What? What is it?" Kenji asked.

"Look at that bird cage. See anything?"

"Nope," Kenji said, puzzled.

"Look again, half-pint."

That's when Tori realized what was in the cage. On the bottom lay a ball of still yellow feathers.

"Oh!" she cried. Instantly, her eyes filled with tears.

Kenji shouted, "Look over there! A pumper! It's a pumper!" Unlike Tori, he wasn't bothered by the sight of a dead canary. But a pumper belching a steady cloud of white smoke—now that's something else. Near the pumper was a fire truck with its hoses lying all over the street like a giant spider-web. Firemen were spraying the nearby rubble.

"Look at those hoses. Lots of water going through them. The pumper's doing its job."

Kenji's delight made Tori smile. This was the first time Tori had been close to a fire and actually saw a pumper working, and it *was* fascinating. She watched the stoker shovel coal through the hatch.

Papa rested his hand on her shoulder. He hadn't said a word since they arrived.

"Papa, look at that," Tori said tugging gently at his sleeve. She pointed to a stand of trees. "Look at those trees, the ones growing along the side of the road."

"I see, Tori," he answered.

"How is that possible, Papa? How could all those trees be OK? Why didn't they burn up like the others?"

"Perhaps they were saved when the wind changed. This must be the very edge of the fire line. They are here now because the wind changed direction very, very fast."

Tori shivered. The fog that had been scarce all summer long had finally made an appearance, covering her like a damp blanket.

"Come on, children. It's getting late. Let's go home."

"Oh, Papa, just a little longer," Kenji begged. "Please."

Kenji's pleading had little effect. Papa took his hand and headed toward the truck. Tori walked slowly after them. Sad thoughts of Fudge alone in the Griffin house flooded her mind and slowed her feet. Only after she had walked a few steps past the shoe-repair shop did she become aware of someone standing in the doorway, barely noticeable in the evening's fragile light.

She kept walking but stopped after a few steps. Something about the figure in the doorway seemed familiar. The faint light made it difficult for Tori to get a good look. But she could see that the dark figure appeared to be a young girl with light hair, and a red-and-white dress. She couldn't see the girl's face because her hands covered her eyes. Suddenly the girl lowered her hands. Tori gasped. The girl's red-eyed and weepy face belonged to none other than Agnes Wetherby.

Chapter Eighteen

❦ Tori ❦

Agnes stood ramrod straight, chin lifted, arms crossed.

"Agnes!" Tori blurted out.

Agnes remained silent. Tori looked around to see if the other Wetherbys were nearby. No one was visible. In fact, now that darkness had finally arrived, the street was nearly deserted. Most of the people who came to watch the fire were several blocks away. Tori continued to walk toward the truck.

She didn't hurry to catch up with Papa and the boys. Something about Agnes standing alone like that slowed her steps. *Why was Agnes crying? Where was her family? Was she waiting for them, or did she run away? Oh, well, it's no concern of mine. Agnes is the last person in the world I want to think about. She's a big girl. She can take care of herself.*

The Bamboo Garden

Just before climbing onto the truck's running board, Tori took a last look back. Was Agnes still there? Had she disappeared? Tori didn't want anything to do with that girl ever again. But one little peek wouldn't hurt. That's when she saw that Agnes had left the shelter of the doorway and was staring at Tori.

"Haruo!" Papa shouted. "Let's see if you have the same luck with the crank this time."

"Righto, Papa." Haruo stood in front of the truck, hands gripping the crank, a mop of black hair nearly covering his eyes.

Tori hoped Haruo's luck would hold. She had to get out of there.

"Remember, son, plant your feet firmly on the ground." Papa encouraged Haruo from the behind the wheel.

As Haruo turned the crank, Papa pushed up the little gear he called the spark. At the same time he pushed down on one of the three floor pedals, all the while mumbling the little rhyme he had taught himself. "Spark up, gas down!" Nothing happened. They tried again. Still nothing.

"That's OK, son," Papa shouted. "Let's give it a rest. We'll try in a few seconds."

Tori didn't want to look back at Agnes, but she couldn't help it. *Please, please, make Agnes go away!*

She turned around to look. Now Agnes stood a few feet from the truck.

Quickly, Tori turned away, pretending to be interested in Papa and Haruo's efforts with the truck. They tried again. *Please, please, work, little truck! Hurry up! Hurry up!* She crossed the fingers on both hands and closed her eyes, just the way Polly had done so many times when she had wished particularly hard for something.

"Don't worry, Haruo," Papa said. "One more crank and I'm sure we'll get it. Just rest your arms a moment. The fourth crank should do it!"

Without looking, Tori knew Agnes stood near the truck. *Is she going to talk to us? What does she want? Why is she standing there? Is she going to say terrible things to us? I'll just ignore her. I'll pretend she doesn't exist. She's invisible to me.*

"Tori, is that you?"

Agnes peered into the truck's window, impossible to ignore. But Tori tried. She didn't reply. She turned her head away, put her hands in her lap, and sat very still. In those brief seconds, Tori became aware of Papa and Haruo watching her.

In a small, wavering voice Agnes said, "Tori?"

Agnes sounded different. The biting, sarcastic tone had disappeared.

"Toriko, is that a friend of yours?" Papa spoke in Japanese, quietly.

"No, Papa. She is *not* a friend."

The need to talk privately with Papa forced her to use Japanese, something she rarely did in front of non-Japanese people.

"But she called you by your name."

"She is *not* a friend," Tori repeated firmly.

"OK, Papa!" Haruo shouted, no longer interested in the stranger. "Let's try again."

Papa muttered quietly to himself as he and Haruo tried to crank up the car for the fourth time, "Spark up, gas down."

Moving her eyes to the right, Tori tried to glimpse Agnes. No red-and-white stripes. *Had she left? What in the world did she want with me? Maybe if I look one more time I can make sure she's disappeared.* Tori turned her head slightly. No Agnes. She looked around more confidently now. Agnes had really left.

The fourth crank didn't work any better than the others. Papa and Haruo silently waited for yet another try.

"Toriko, why didn't you speak to that girl?" Papa asked, looking straight ahead, his hands on the steering wheel. "She looks upset. This is not like you. I am surprised."

Tori remained silent. She looked down, pretending to brush away something off her skirt. Papa's words stung. But he wouldn't understand. He had no idea about Agnes. Still, Tori thought he was right about one thing. Agnes did look upset. She'd been crying. Where was her family? What could have happened? The fire! Of course, that's it! The fire must have something to do with Agnes Wetherby standing alone in the night. Then Tori did something she could hardly believe. She opened the truck door.

"I'll be right back, Papa."

Papa nodded.

She walked toward Agnes, who hadn't gone very far.

"Agnes, wait!" she called.

With each step, Tori's legs felt shakier. She wasn't sure what to expect, but knowing that Papa was nearby helped.

"What do you want?" Tori asked.

Silence.

"What do you want?" Tori asked again, baffled by Agnes's strange behavior.

Tears over-flowed Agnes's red-rimmed eyes.

"What is it, Agnes?" she asked, her voice softening just a bit.

"Oh, I just don't know what to do."

"What do you mean?"

"I've lost my family."

"What do you mean you've lost your family?"

"We were all together one minute. But with the fire and all, when I left the house they were gone. They just vanished. I've looked everywhere, but I can't find them! It's just like them to go off and forget all about me."

Agnes's words poured out now, along with more tears. Tori could scarcely believe the Agnes standing before her. Gone was the mean and hateful girl whose words cut so deeply.

"I don't know what to do, or where to go. Golly, I'm so hungry, too."

Tori heard the truck's engine roar to life. She knew if Papa didn't get moving right away it would stall. Desperately she wondered what Polly would do in her place. She'd probably take Agnes back to the truck and tell Papa to take them home. Polly wouldn't even think twice about it. But this was Agnes. The idea of Agnes Wetherby in her house was too horrible for words.

"Maybe they'll come back and look for you. Maybe you need to wait a little longer," Tori suggested hopefully.

"I've been standing here forever! I think they've forgotten all about me."

"How'd this happen?"

"Oh, everything was so mixed up. I mean, when the house caught on fire, Mother got hysterical. She was running everywhere, but she didn't seem to know what to do. We'd been waiting forever for Father's workmen to pick us up along with our stuff. You know, the things we put on the porch. They never came. The roof caught on fire. Most of the top floor, too. We all ran out of the house."

The truck's horn interrupted them.

"Come on. Let's talk to my father."

Tori watched Agnes hesitate for a fraction of a second before following her to the sputtering truck.

"Papa, this is Agnes Wetherby," Tori said once she and Agnes were seated. "Her house burned down and she can't find her family."

"Hello, Agnes," Papa said, looking straight ahead, hands tightly clutching the shaking steering wheel. "We shall talk after we get this truck moving. I do not want it to stall again."

While Papa drove slowly along University Avenue, Agnes told her story over again. Fresh tears ran down her cheeks when she got to the part about how her mother, brother, and sister had run out of the house without her.

"I only went back in to get my new scarf. The wind was blowing so hard I thought it'd be good to have with me. By the time I came back, they were gone!"

The Bamboo Garden

Before she could stop herself, Tori blurted out the question that haunted her now. "Did Polly's house burn, too?"

"I don't know. It seemed like all the houses on Spruce Street were on fire. I ran toward town. Houses were burning all around me. It was so scary."

Tori had her answer. The Griffins' beautiful home and sweet Fudge were surely gone, turned into a pile of rubble and ash. Tears threatened to spill down her cheeks.

Papa continued driving, but slowly. Tori guessed he was trying to figure out what to do with Agnes.

Haruo, overhearing their conversation from the truck bed, poked his head through the window. "Papa, ask a policeman to help the girl."

His idea didn't surprise Tori. Haruo was always keen on talking to the police.

Tori tried to picture Papa explaining everything to a policeman. His English was good but his words got jumbled when he was nervous. Papa said nothing. As they puttered past the university, Tori remembered something Millie told them, something that might help.

"Papa! Turn left here, and drive onto campus. I have an idea!"

Papa did as she asked. Inching up the main road he steered the truck in the direction of the university buildings poised on a slight rise.

"What's your idea, Toriko?" Papa asked as they drew closer to the center of campus.

"Donald's girlfriend, Millie, told us how the girls were helping out, something about setting up a place for lost children."

Tori glanced at Agnes. No more tears.

"That is a good idea, Toriko! Where should I go?"

"Just park by the Campanile, Papa. It's right there!" she said, pointing to the huge tower at the end of the road.

There were lots of other cars parked on campus along with huge piles of furniture in unexpected places. People were walking everywhere and, although Tori had never been on the campus at night, she was sure it had never looked like this before. Standing by the base of the Campanile, Tori had a good view of the hills lit by fire's red glow.

Tori quickly found the student union building. Not long ago, Polly had shown Tori the ink fountain where students filled up their pens. The place bubbled with activity. Papa, the boys, and Agnes followed her to a set of tables outside the building.

"Excuse me," Tori said to a girl sitting at one.

A man's tweed jacket covered the girl's shoulders. Tori realized how cool the night had become. After so many hot days and nights, the chilly air felt good.

"Is this where we report a missing person?"

"Why, yes, dear. Are you lost?" the coed asked, wrapping the jacket tighter around her bare arms.

"No, not me, but my friend here," she answered, nudging Agnes to the front of their little group.

"Well, tell us your name, honey," the coed said to Agnes. "We'll see what we can do for you."

Relief swept over Tori as she listened to Agnes tell her story punctuated with tears and trembling voice. They would help Agnes. Tori and her family could go home. Tori couldn't wait. There was no telling how long Agnes would remain this polite. Any second she could turn into the mean neighbor girl. Just a few more minutes and they'd be rid of her.

Agnes's elbow bumped Tori's ribs.

"Tori, did you hear what she asked you?"

Tori looked at Agnes, then at the girl before her. "What?" she asked, feeling silly.

"Could you and your family take care of Agnes tonight?" the coed asked, obviously for a second time.

The question left Tori speechless. Agnes Wetherby to spend the night in her home? This couldn't be happening. She looked at Papa standing behind her, his hands resting on the boys' shoulders.

He had heard and understood the question. Nodding he said, "We would be pleased to have the young lady at our—"

A nearby shout interrupted him.

"Agnes!"

Tori knew the voice belonged to Mrs. Wetherby.

"Mother!"

"Agnes, we've been looking everywhere for you. Where *have* you been?"

"Mother, oh, Mother, how could you have left me like that? What happened? Where did you go?"

Tori watched mother and daughter exchange a quick hug. She couldn't move. A second ago she'd been horrified that Papa would agree to have Agnes Wetherby at her home. Now, quite suddenly, she felt useless and discarded.

Mrs. Wetherby fussed over Agnes, all the while brushing bits of gray, sooty flakes off her daughter's shoulders and hair. Tori looked at Papa. Silently, he signaled it was time to go.

Mrs. Wetherby and Agnes were too absorbed to notice. Agnes repeated the story of her awful day, going on and on as if Tori never existed. *How silly of me to get all worried about this selfish and mean girl,* thought Tori as she followed Papa back to the truck. They were just about to climb in when a shout broke into her dark thoughts.

"Tori, wait!"

She turned to see Agnes running in her direction, pulling her mother by the hand. The scowl on

Mrs. Wetherby's face worried Tori. Now what? What could they possibly want?

"Tori, I . . . " Agnes said.

Tori remained silent.

"I just wanted to say—"

Mrs. Wetherby interrupted Agnes, clearly displeased with her daughter. "Hurry up, dear. Your father is waiting!"

"I just wanted to say . . . thanks."

"OK, Agnes, now let's go," Mrs. Wetherby said impatiently.

Before Tori could answer, they were gone. It didn't matter. Words were lost to Tori. The shock was too great. Agnes Wetherby had said something nice.

Chapter Nineteen

⚕ Polly ⚕

Why is someone sitting on her chest? Polly's head hurts, too. A sheet is twisted around her body in a tight hug. But a single whiff of burnt wood jogs her memory: the fire and Fudge. The most vivid memory of all was Mother's face peering at her–white as a sheet, worry etched deep on her forehead.

Polly opens her eyes. Morning sun fills her bedroom even though the curtains are closed. Next to the bed sits Mother, asleep in the rocker, the purple-and-blue afghan on her lap. As soon as Polly turns over for a better look, Mother awakes.

"Polly! You're up!"

"I guess so," she croaks, surprised by her dry, sandpapery throat.

"You've been sleeping a long time."

"I have?"

The Bamboo Garden

"Ever since we tucked you into bed yesterday," Mother says, handing Polly a glass of water. "Here, drink this. I'll be right back."

As soon as Mother returns with a breakfast tray, Polly showers her with questions. "Was the fire all a bad dream? Why does my chest hurt? How did you find me?" But one question seems most important. "Did you find Fudge?"

Mother will have none of it. "I'm very angry at you, young lady!"

"You are?"

"Yes, I am! You're lucky to be alive! Do you realize that?"

"Yes, ma'am."

"You should never have run off like that! You took a very foolish chance! You could have been killed!"

Mother speaks quietly, but Polly knows she's furious. "Don't you ever do anything like that again! Do you hear me! Not ever again!"

"Yes, ma'am."

"When I couldn't find you, I was beside myself. How could you do that to me?"

"I'm sorry, Mother. It's just that—"

"No, Polly. No talking. Just listen!"

Polly deserves this lecture. Luckily, Polly's sudden coughing fit interrupts Mother. When Polly finally stops, Mother's anger is gone.

"Now, Polls, you have to eat something!"

"But I can't."

"Just sip some orange juice. I know that's what Dr. Layton will tell you when he gets here. Drink lots of fluids."

"Yes, ma'am."

After a few swallows, Polly looks closely at Mother. There are creases around the corners of her mouth Polly never noticed before. Wild blond curls spring out in every direction. From Mother's puffy eyes, Polly guesses she didn't sleep too well. After a few sips, Polly once again asks about Fudge.

"Polly, we can't find her. We've looked everywhere."

"I won't ever be able to eat again." Polly moans, handing back the glass. "Not if we don't find Fudge. Where could she be?"

"Maybe she's just hiding somewhere, Polls."

"Knock, knock," Father says, peeking into Polly's bedroom. "Can a gentleman visit his favorite little girl?"

"Oh, Father, any luck yet? Did you find her?"

Briskly, Father walks into the room and seats himself on the edge of the bed. He takes her hands in his.

"Look, Polls, I've searched in all of Fudge's favorite spots. Outside, too. But frankly, that bunny is gone. I know it's hard, but we have to accept the fact that

Fudge got out during the fire. She probably didn't make it."

Polly doesn't want to admit Father may be right. Fudge must have run away. But maybe she survived, just like their house. After Father and Mother finally leave, Polly decides to take a quick peek at her neighborhood. Mother won't approve, but Polly has to see how Spruce Street looks. Frightening images of burning houses ran through her head all morning. Is their house the only one not burned up? One look, then she'll hop right back into bed.

Slowly she parts the curtains, then quickly lets them fall closed. There must be something wrong with her eyes. She blinks a few times and opens the curtains again. Fire can't do that! Did a bomb explode out there? Spruce Street is gone — the trees, houses, cars, even Mr. Applegate's prize roses, and, of course, the Wetherby house. She saw that yesterday, when it got swallowed up by flames. Today, only charred bits of rubble remain. Feeling guilty, she looks up at the hills now. All the houses are gone, wiped away as if by an enormous evil hand. She stares. Chimneys and fireplaces are the only things left standing. A few people wander about aimlessly. Cars and trolleys are gone, and in their place lay piles of smoldering bricks. Two soldiers in brown uniforms walk by her house.

Rifles rest on their shoulders; boots are laced high and tight. What are they doing here?

Trying to make sense of everything makes Polly's head spin. Did the whole town burn down? She runs to the sleeping porch for a peek through the canvas rolls. Amazed, she sees that Jerry's place is fine and so are all the homes on his block.

Later in the morning, Dr. Layton stops by with his scary black bag. He keeps all kinds of unpleasant surprises inside. Will he give her a shot like the time she stepped on a nail? Only his stethoscope comes out this morning. She doesn't mind the cold metal on her chest. He listens carefully, thumps her back and tells her to take a few deep breaths. Surprisingly, this makes her cough. Why does her chest hurt, too?

"Hmmmmm," he mutters to himself now and again. Mother stands nearby, talking nonstop.

"You see, Dr. Layton, I was absolutely frantic, looking for her. The police wouldn't let me go anywhere. But then, when things quieted down, I convinced one of them to take me home. They drove me right to the front door. There she was, asleep or maybe unconscious on her bed. I really don't know which. She came back for her bunny, you know. There was black soot around her nose and mouth. Oh, and she's been here ever since."

Mother stops for a moment, takes a deep breath,

and gives Polly a look that makes her squirm. "Anyhow," she goes on, "she slept pretty much through the night."

"Well," Dr. Layton says, standing up at last. He places the stethoscope in his black bag, snapping it shut. "Well, well."

He turns to Polly, speaking to her in a very serious tone. His deep voice rumbles like far-away thunder. "Now listen to me, young lady. You have a fair amount of black smoke in your lungs. I imagine you ran all the way to your house, eh?"

"Yes, sir, very fast," she adds, thinking this might be important.

"Well, you are a lucky little girl. You'll be just fine in a day or so. Just do what your mother tells you, rest, and drink plenty of fluids."

Turning to Mother, he continues, "I guess the whole town's lucky, in a manner of speaking. Even though all those thousands of people lost their homes, I don't think we've had one fatality! Amazing! Almost six hundred homes burned down in a little over two hours, and not one death. Of course, we've had plenty of minor injuries from people taking foolish chances, but I don't think one person fell off a roof! There were a whole lot of darn fools standing up there watering down their houses with hoses. Yep, I'd say we've all been pretty lucky!"

Polly knows she was one of those "darn fools" climbing out on a roof. But it worked! It worked!

Mainly she tries to follow Dr. Layton's orders. But with so much going on downstairs, she just can't stand the thought of missing out on anything. She hops out of bed to stand in the doorway listening, and then runs back when she hears someone coming up the stairs.

None of the telephones are working, so lots of neighbors drop by. Some are crying. They've lost everything in the fire. Others come to see about Polly. She hears Mother thank them for their concern. "All she needs are a few days of rest to clear up those lungs," she repeats over and over. As each neighbor leaves, Mother adds, "I know she'll appreciate your keeping an eye out for Fudge. She's worried sick about her bunny."

Bored and fidgety, Polly decides to send a message to Jerry, and maybe tell him about her adventure. But first she'd better check the rope on the bucket-phone. Did the fire burn it up? Nope; the rope is fine and the bucket is right where she left it during that big wind. But what's in the bottom? Something brown, furry and very still! Could it be? Polly doesn't dare breathe. Squatting close to the bucket, she knows! It's Fudge! But why so quiet? Polly gets as close as possible. "Fudge, is that you? Are you OK?"

The Bamboo Garden

As if on cue, Fudge lifts her head, blinks her big blue eyes, and touches her wet cold nose to Polly's! With great care, Polly lifts the bunny from the bucket, hugging and kissing her.

"Fudge, it's you!" Polly whispers, burying her face in the bunny's soft fur. "You didn't burn up after all! I've been so worried about you!" She breathes in Fudge's sweet lavender-like scent now with a hint of smoke.

Her excited shouts bring Mother and Father as well as everyone else in the house hurrying upstairs — Jerry, his mom, and Professor Cole. There's lots of laughter; Fudge has been in the house all along!

After each person greets Fudge, Polly is back in bed. Everyone wants to talk. Polly loves having her room filled like this. While the grownups are busy talking, Jerry makes himself comfortable on the edge of her bed. Together they stroke Fudge's chocolate brown coat. The bunny buries herself in Polly's lap as if to say, "I'm back where I belong, safe at last!"

"I just don't know how we all forgot about Fudge," Jerry wonders aloud. "I know we had to leave in a hurry, but *Fudge!* Jeepers!"

Polly can't help thinking how the terrible fight with Tori might have had something to do with it. Awful Agnes sure didn't help.

"Father and Mother are pretty mad at me."

"Yeah, you shouldn't have come back like that."

"But then I saved the house, didn't I?"

"That's what they say."

"No, really, I did! But I'll tell you something. Walking out on that roof was the scariest thing I've ever done."

"You were pretty brave, Polly. Guess you must be some kind of hero."

"You think so?"

"Yeah, I do. But, hey, Professor Cole's sort of a hero, too!" Polly looks at the professor. He is so busy whispering to Mrs. Berman, he doesn't hear the compliment. "He helped me load some of our things into his car. We left just in time. Parked at the university. He found Mom, too! What a night! But this morning we had to get the car back. It's a good thing we did. Right, Mom? Tell them about the roadblocks."

"Oh, that's right, dear," Mrs. Berman says. "The police and army set up roadblocks all around the fire area early this morning. From now on we can't get in or out of the neighborhood without a pass. For that you have to go downtown and wait in long lines."

"It's true," says Jerry. "We got back just before those barricades went up."

"I didn't know about this, Lawrence," Father says.

"Seems the authorities are worried about looters,"

Professor Cole says. "But frankly, Bernard, there's not much to loot."

"There's no telling what the fire missed," Mrs. Berman chimes in. "Why, people are already going through what's left of their homes looking for jewelry, or even melted silver and gold. Early this morning I saw one of the hoboes doing just that over at the Wetherbys'. I must say, he sure seemed to be enjoying himself. He didn't stop grinning the whole time I watched him."

Polly and Jerry exchange glances. Smilin' Sam! Who else? Then guilt washes over Polly. Jerry knows her wish. Is that what happened? Her wish made the Wetherby house burn to the ground?

"Oh, yes, the Wetherbys. They must be devastated," Mother says.

"That may be true, dear," Father agrees, "but if I know Mr. Wetherby, he'll be the first to rebuild. He's a shrewd businessman, probably one of the fortunate ones with fire insurance. Oh, they'll rebuild all right. It's bound to be something far grander than their old house."

A few minutes later the adults leave, still talking about the fire.

"Jerry, tell me everything," Polly begs, as soon as they are alone. "Tell me about your great adventure and I'll tell you all about mine."

Jerry settles into the corner rocker. Tipping back and forth a few times, he remains quiet, grinning.

"Oh, come on, Jerry! Tell me!"

"Whoa! What's the hurry?"

"Please! Pretty please, with sugar on it?"

"OK, hold your horses." After a few more rocks and teasing smiles, he begins.

"So, after I left you to get my own things, I must have been racing around our apartment trying to figure out what to do when Professor Cole came in. He asked if I needed help. I think he knew Mom was at work. Maybe he heard me running around. Anyhow, we only had a few minutes. Turns out I didn't need to do that at all! Slept in my own bed, just like you!"

"You slept in your house last night?"

"Sure."

"Were you afraid the fire would come back?"

"Well, that's the miracle of it all, Polly! We got to campus all right, and of course there were tons of other people, too. You must have seen that."

"Tons! I've never seen anything like it!"

"Professor Cole thought we might have to spend the night there. The fire was huge. We had a great view. Everyone thought it'd burn through the night. Well, around four-thirty in the afternoon, all that changed!"

"What are you talking about?"

"All of a sudden the wind shifted. It stopped blowing the fire downtown. That's where it was headed, you know."

"Wow!"

"But that's not all! The wind brought something special with it."

"What?"

"Soggy air from the bay! Just what we needed!"

"Jeepers, Jerry. Sure does sound like a miracle!"

"Once those winds came up, the fire was pretty much over. Then the three of us walked home."

"Three of you?"

"Yeah. Professor Cole, Mom, and me."

"But how'd your mother find you?"

"Easy. I stayed with everything and Professor Cole walked to Hinks. They were just closing up for the day. Turns out Mom was worried about me. But she had to stay 'til they decided to shut down."

"That was real nice of Professor Cole to help you out like that."

"He's terrif, Polly! Mom thinks he's swell, too."

Jerry stays for the rest of the morning until Mother tells him Polly needs to rest. By dinner Polly feels so good Mother lets her eat downstairs. Best of all, Mother says Polly can go outside the next day, as long as she doesn't overdo it.

That night the bucket phone gets a lively workout.

Messages about the next day fly back and forth. On her last note of the evening, Polly writes about something that has been nagging at her all day.

Dear Jerry,
    Did your wish come true yet? By the way, what was it? I'm not sure about mine. The Wetherbys are gone. But they may come back. Do you know Tori's wish?
                    Your Friends,
                    Polly and Fudge

Next to Fudge's name she draws a picture of a bunny's paw. Holding the message in front of her, she knows something is missing—but what? The red crayon catches her eye. That's it! Carefully, she outlines the paw with a big red heart.

Chapter Twenty

☞ Polly ☜

"**N**ow Polly, you and Jerry be careful! Remember, you promised to take it easy. That means no running, and don't go too far up the hill."

"Don't worry," Polly says, making herself eat the last bite of scrambled eggs. Mother will never let her go if she doesn't finish everything on her plate. "I'll be extra careful. We'll be back before you know it!"

Polly likes having meals in the dining room with everyone. Of course, the big table and oversized chairs are great for hiding Fudge on her lap. No one notices. She has vowed to never let the bunny out of her sight ever again.

Donald is cramming one of Mrs. Hastings's biscuits into his mouth. He sure looks a lot cleaner today. Polly is glad the biscuit keeps him from talking. Yesterday, he went on and on about how he and his chums managed to save their fraternity house. The other story he must have told a zillion times was about the Dwight Club. Saved from the flames Sunday night, it became a pile of ashes the next day.

Millie is also at the table. Too bad her apartment burned up. But that means Polly will have a roommate until Millie finds another place. Of course, Aunt Charlotte and Uncle Horace are here, too. They have nowhere else to go.

Polly has never seen her house like this. Bed linens and blankets are scattered in every room. She loves all the commotion, although waiting in line for the bathroom isn't much fun. Still, no one complains.

Aunt Charlotte doesn't say anything at breakfast. Even though she asked how Polly felt, Polly can tell there are other things on her mind. Uncle Horace never talks anyhow, so Polly doesn't pay much attention to him, except she can't help noticing he looks thinner, and more unhappy than usual. His moustache is droopier and his few wisps of hair stick out here and there.

Much of the conversation at the table is about how to get a pass. Polly wonders if the soldiers will stop her from going in and out of her neighborhood without one. After all, she's just a kid.

She especially enjoys hearing Father read the ads from the morning paper. "Miss Mary Morris, formerly of 2335 Cedar Street, would be grateful if the young man who helped carry her clothes would let her know where they are. 2631 Webster Street."

Donald muffles a laugh.

"That poor woman," Mother says, giving him a stern look.

"Hmmm, well, I'm sure there was lots of confusion," Father mutters. "That must have been a common occurrence."

Polly knows he still feels terrible about not being around to help out. He hasn't disappeared into his study for two days now. While she was stuck in bed, Father told her all about his ride home that Monday. The five o'clock ferry from San Francisco was filled with other men just like him, all anxious to get home to their families. The hardest part was that helpless feeling, he said, watching the fire and smoke cover the Berkeley hills as the ferry made its slow journey home. Getting back to the house took forever. He had to walk most of the way.

"Confusion—yes, Bernard, I'd say there was plenty of that," Aunt Charlotte agrees.

Polly glances at Aunt Charlotte. Losing her house was terrible, but a stupid mistake bothered her most—grabbing the Mah-Jongg box instead of her jewelry box. But with flames everywhere, she had only seconds before the fire pushed her out. Polly guesses the carved ivory game tiles aren't worth nearly as much as silver, gold, and precious gems. Polly made a mistake, too. She understands.

"The ladies from the Unitarian Church want to sponsor a community shower for families who lost everything," Mother says. "You know, try to replace some of their things." She looks up from her plate. "Charlotte, would you like me to put your name on the list? We'll probably start hosting the showers next week."

"That won't be necessary, Dot," Aunt Charlotte replies stiffly.

Then, in a more familiar tone, "We're going to rebuild, you know. Our main concern now is finding an architect who will help. But they're all so busy now."

Without looking up from his paper Father says to no one in particular, "Let's hope the architects design fireproof homes this time around."

Polly and Jerry get a late start. First, Fudge is tucked away on the sleeping porch, pink blanket carefully placed in her favorite spot under the desk. Then Polly makes sure everyone knows she'll be gone, reminding them to keep an eye out for Fudge.

The changes in the neighborhood shock Polly. Even though there are lots of people out and about, they are eerily quiet. A spicy smoke smell lingers in the air. After a few minutes, Polly realizes her armpits are wet and sticky. Memories of running of Spruce Street flash through her mind—mostly of houses being swallowed by orange flames.

An explosion thunders in the distance. She grabs Jerry's arm but then lets go, embarrassed. If he's not worried, what's the matter with her?

"What was that?"

"Dynamite," he answers calmly.

"Dynamite?"

"Yep."

"What for?"

"Professor Cole told me all about it this morning. He heard about it from the soldiers, about how the fire department is going to dynamite those walls and chimneys—anything that didn't fall down after being burned. They're pretty dangerous."

"Let's go watch," Polly says, her fears now gone. Watching chimneys blow up sounds like fun.

"Don't think so, Polly. I promised your mother we wouldn't go too far. She'll have my head if we go up the hill, and that's where they're starting to dynamite, up at the top where the fire started."

"Let's just see how far we can get, Jerry. Please," Polly begs, putting on her cheeriest smile.

A fine snow-white ash covers the streets and empty lots. Chunks of melted metal block parts of the sidewalk and the dirt road.

"Jer, let's play a game. Let's see if we can guess what some of the burned-up things used to be!"

They come to a big chunk of metal with a still-recognizable fender attached.

"I know this one, Polly. It's a burned-up automobile!"

"Righto. Say, what about that? Too little for an automobile."

Polly points to a pile of small metal chunks, some with wire coils, like frizzy hair sticking out.

Jerry doesn't seem to know. Polly can't figure it out either. Then she sees Mrs. Crawford weeping over another one.

"I think I know what they are," Polly whispers.

"Yeah, me too," Jerry says in a hushed voice. "She must have pushed her piano outside somehow, before the fire came."

"But the fire found it anyways."

After that, Polly spots several other piano skeletons along the way. Then came the biggest surprise of all. On the sidewalk is an upright piano, its highly polished wood shining in the morning sun. The instrument looks perfect, not even a scratch.

"Jerry, how's this possible?"

She knows she can always count on him for reasonable explanations about strange things. He rubs his chin, just the way Professor Cole did that time Polly asked him about hoboes.

"I'm not sure. Of course, the fire did miss lots of things. You saw that. Look at your house. Hardly a scratch. Then there are houses where everything else around them burned to the ground, even the trees and telephone poles. I don't think anyone knows why."

Getting to the top of the hill isn't so important now. The explosions no longer scare her. But the faces of all those families sifting through the ashes of what used to be their homes makes her feel sad. The grown-ups are working hard with their poking and digging. Occasionally, one of them shouts and holds up some small object. The others come running. Children play nearby. Polly can't help smiling at a little girl playing in a bathtub surrounded by piles of rubble.

The farther they walk, the worse the smell. Who would have guessed that burnt houses could stink like this? Her nose and throat starts to hurt. Where firemen emptied their hoses to wet glowing bricks and smoldering debris, the smell is even worse. The empty lots with stairs-to-nowhere fascinate her most.

"Hey, I've got an idea."

Jerry grimaces. "It better not get us into trouble."

"Oh, come on! When have my ideas ever gotten us into trouble?" Polly knows her innocent look doesn't fool him.

He laughs hard; she thinks maybe a little too hard. "OK. What's your idea?"

"I just have to see something that isn't burned up. Let's go to Codornices Creek, just for a little bit. I'll bet it smells better than this—just what the doctor ordered."

Luckily the fire missed their favorite spot. Water gurgles over the rocks the way it always has. The shade of the oak trees lining the bank never looked more beautiful. It's as if the fire never happened.

Sitting next to Jerry, toes dangling in the cool water, Polly hears leaves rustling in the nearby bushes. She looks at Jerry. He must have heard, too. Instead of a squirrel, Smilin' Sam emerges from the bushes. His hands brush something away from his eyes.

"Darn spiders! I jest don't know why they have to build their webs where they're always in the way," he says, smiling all the time. When the little man spots Polly, his smile grows even bigger.

"Say, Jerry, look who's here."

Jerry doesn't seem interested, but then, he never did warm up to Smilin' Sam. She waves to the little man without thinking. Suddenly she realizes she doesn't know how she feels about him. Before the fire, she really wanted to talk to him about the wooden nickel. Now, after hearing about Smilin' Sam digging around the Wetherby place, she's not so sure.

The Bamboo Garden

"Why, if it isn't Polly and Jerry! How're you two? Where's Tori?"

Not waiting for an answer he sits nearby, and removes his well-worn boots. Polly tries not to stare at his grubby socks with holes big enough for several of his toes to poke through. After taking off his socks, Smilin' Sam eases his over-sized feet into the cold, fast-moving stream.

"We're fine, thanks," Polly says. "Oh, and about Tori. She doesn't live near here, you know. Maybe someday she will. I'm always hoping for that."

Polly listens to these familiar words—her wish for Tori to be her neighbor. That loophole! She had wanted to tell Tori about it so badly. But then the fight, the fire—she never had a chance. Then the Wetherby house *did* go up in smoke, just like Polly wished. Did she make the wrong kind of wish, the kind Professor Cole said could bring bad luck? She'd been trying to push this thought away for days. But now it's back.

"Hey, guess what?" Polly says, eager to change the subject. "Jerry's house didn't burn down. Isn't that terrif? Neither did mine."

"Well, that's mighty good, yep, that's just grand. You two are lucky."

"That's for sure," she agrees.

"Matter of fact, this town is pretty lucky!"

"What do you mean?"

"If it weren't for me and my buddies, the whole place might have gone up in flames."

His eyes begin to shine just like Father's before he tells a big yarn. Polly suspects he's exaggerating, but curiosity gets the better of her.

"How'd you save the town?"

"Why, young lady, we helped put out one of the biggest fires!"

"You did?"

"Yep, sure did—right downtown, in one of those fancy hat shops. We held the hoses for the firemen."

"You mean the fire reached downtown after all?"

Polly is amazed that the fire had spread that far.

"Yep, a bit of it did. Good thing we were there to help." He pauses for a brief instant before announcing, "Problem is, Berkeley doesn't seem quite so appealing to me anymore."

"Why?" Polly asks, aware that Jerry has become very still.

Smilin' Sam takes time to study his wet toes before talking.

"Well, young lady, it's simple. With plenty of homes 'round here, I had lots of work. People would hire me to do this an' that, give me a good meal."

"But now lots of those homes are gone, is that it, Sam?"

"Yep. I'm giving serious thought to movin' on."

"Where will you go?" Jerry asks, his first words since the little man showed up.

"Winter's coming. I don't much care for the cold. I'm thinking of going south — Santa Barbara, maybe. Spent some mighty nice days there a few years back. Yep, Santa Barbara sounds good to me."

He removes his cap and scratches his head.

"Are you going to ride the rails there?" Polly imagines him sitting in the boxcar with his other hobo friends.

"Nat'urlly," he says lying down on the packed earth, his ragged cap for a pillow.

Polly also lies down, hands behind her head, toes still under water.

The blue sky is dotted with wispy clouds, some shaped like nearly perfect circles, just like the wooden nickel. Should she let Smilin' Sam know what Professor Cole told them? Should she tell him about her wish? Oh, why not!

"Say, we still have that wooden nickel you gave us. We've all taken turns holding on to it. Tori's got it now."

"That's nice."

"I'm thinking that maybe it's magical or something. What do you think?"

When Smilin' Sam doesn't say anything, Polly wonders if maybe he didn't hear. In a louder voice, she says, "So, I've been thinking that wooden nickel is special."

"I'll say it is," agrees Smilin' Sam. "That wood is *gen-u-ine* oak. Tough to carve."

"No, I mean, could it have special powers?"

Smilin' Sam sits up, pulling his feet from the water. Reaching into the sack of clothes at his side, he takes out a plaid flannel shirt for drying his toes. But, still he doesn't answer Polly.

She tries to be quiet, to wait patiently. Silently, she watches him stow the slightly damp shirt back in the sack. About to burst, Polly's words finally tumble out.

"When I had the nickel I wished for something really hard, but nothing happened. Well, something did happen, but not what I expected. I don't know if my wish came true or not."

Quietly, Smilin' Sam pulls on his socks, then laces up his boots. Once on his feet, he hikes up his trousers. For the first time Polly sees that they are held up by a rope belt. Expertly, he quickly ties his sack to the carved walking stick. Finally, he looks at Polly.

"Don't know nothin' about wishes, young lady." He

pauses to scratch his beard. "Well now, that's not exactly true. I make wishes all the time, like I wish I had a steak for dinner, or wish I could sleep in a soft bed, or my favorite—wish I had a few more bucks in my pocket. But wishes are just that—wishes. Now, I'd much rather spend my time eatin' berries, coolin' my feet in this here water, or maybe chattin' with my buddies. Say, that sounds good. Think that's just what I'll do," he says, hoisting the stick onto his shoulder.

"It's been great seeing you, Smilin' Sam," Polly says cheerily, trying to hide her disappointment. But she still can't let go of the nickel subject.

"We'll take good care of the wooden nickel. I think we'll hide it in our bamboo garden. I have just the right little tobacco tin for it. We'll bury it. Maybe make a map just like pirates used to do. That way only the three of us will know where to find it."

"Tell you what, little miss," Smilin' Sam says, the sack swinging a little. "It's a mighty fine nickel and I worked hard on it. Why don't you just give it away? It'd be a shame to bury it. Know what I mean?"

"Yeah, I guess you're right," Polly says, sorry she even mentioned the coin.

Before she can ask another question, Smilin' Sam grins and turns toward town. With just a few steps he is quickly hidden by the dense bushes guarding the creek.

Jerry breaks the silence the little man left behind. "Come on, Polly, let's go home."

"But Jerry, what do you think about all of this? Do you think Professor Cole was just teasing us with all his talk about hoboes and charmed nickels?"

"No, Professor Cole wouldn't do that. Besides, even if your wish didn't come true, maybe Tori's did."

"I guess you're right." Polly doesn't bring up the big fight. Maybe Jerry didn't even notice, being busy with his crystal set and all. Of course, there's always the possibility that Tori doesn't want to be her friend any more.

"Say, you never did tell me if your wish came true. Did it?" Polly asks.

Jerry stops walking before answering. "Naw. Well, maybe. Oh, shucks. I don't know. We'll just have to see," he stammers, digging the toe of his shoe into a pile of leaves. Is he trying to keep from smiling?

"What's going on, Jerry Berman? What *was* your wish?"

"Oh, come on. Sometimes it's better not to talk too much about wishes or they won't come true. You know that."

Chapter Twenty-One

❦ Tori ❦

The day after the fire, Tori felt like her old self but still couldn't go to school because the city had decided to close them for a while. Ordinarily, it would have been great, but thoughts of Polly and Jerry made her fidgety. Why did she yell at Polly like that? Now nothing seemed more important than her friends. Calling them on the telephone was no use, not when Polly's and Jerry's homes were nothing but piles of ashes. Of course that didn't stop her from trying. All she got was busy, busy, and more busy.

Mama finally lost patience with her.

"Toriko, settle down. You are making me nervous with your pacing and worried looks."

"But Mama, what if the Griffins need us? You told Mrs. Griffin we could help. Maybe they need a place to stay. They could stay here. What if they need food and water? We could bring them something. We need to find them. Please, Mama," Tori pleaded.

That had gone on for most of the day. Mama said she was sure they were fine. Hadn't Polly and Mrs. Griffin escaped from the fire? Besides, the city was sure to be helping people. But Tori was certain the Griffins needed them.

All morning Mama worked on sewing dresses for her new customers, friends of Mrs. Griffin. But Tori couldn't keep from pestering her. After the tenth time asking for permission to go to Spruce Street, Mama put her hands over her ears. She had never done that before.

Tori tried to keep busy, even offering to play a game of pickup sticks with Haruo. He looked surprised. He was usually the one begging for a game.

"I won again. That makes six out of six." Haruo laughed as he scooped up the thin sticks, jamming them into their cardboard tube, then scattering them on the ground for a new game.

Tori rarely lost, but today she couldn't concentrate. Haruo freed the yellow stick with a trick she'd taught him.

"I've just got to think of something I can do for Polly and Jerry. They need me," Tori fretted. Haruo won most of the sticks.

"Don't be such a worrywart! Besides, what could you do?"

"You moved, Haruo! My turn."

Carefully, Tori freed a blue stick.

"I'd think of something to . . . oh golly, there goes the red one! Your turn."

The day passed too slowly. Night was worse. Restless, Tori kept getting tangled in her sheet. Every time her eyes closed, gigantic orange and red flames appeared.

The next morning Mama was smiling again. Guiltily, Tori wondered if that had something to do with the schools being reopened. Mama hurried Tori and the boys through breakfast, occasionally glancing at the pile of unfinished dresses waiting on the dining room table. Tori understood. This work was even more important now, without the Griffin house to clean. Next to her lunch pail was the note Mama wrote for Miss Chantrelle, explaining Tori's absence. Tucking it into her dress pocket along with the pennies Mama left for milk, Tori's hand brushed against the wooden nickel Jerry had given her. She'd forgotten about it.

Usually Tori walked to school well behind the boys. Today Haruo hung back. For some reason Tori didn't mind. Haruo had been unusually quiet these last few days, and different somehow. Like yesterday, after winning all the games of pickup sticks, he didn't even boast to Kenji.

They walked in silence for a few blocks. The air was fresh and cool, with hardly any of that nasty smoke smell. A few mothers were out pushing baby buggies. Absentmindedly, Tori drew the wooden nickel from her pocket.

"Can I see?" Haruo held out his hand.

Tori gave it to him.

"What'd you wish for? Did it come true yet?"

His face showed no sign of a smile or smirk. Should she tell him? Haruo seemed really interested. Suddenly embarrassed, Tori realized she couldn't. What a silly wish! How could she have wished for friends? She had wished for a real, true friend—someone who liked her, who'd stick up for her, who'd want to know everything about her. Polly and Jerry really *were* her friends. Didn't Polly talk back to Agnes when they were loading the Griffin car? Didn't Polly look close to punching Agnes? If Mrs. Griffin hadn't shown up, she might have socked the daylights out of that girl. Didn't she remember to give Tori the licorice stick in the middle of everything? And what about Jerry? He was always kind to her. Lots of times he seemed to know exactly what she was thinking, even before

she did. Maybe this coin was lucky after all! Or . . .
maybe they'd *always* been her friends.

Tori smiled. She didn't need this nickel! She got
what she wished for, but Polly and Jerry could sure
use some of its magic. That's when Tori knew what
to do.

Haruo tapped her arm. "Did you hear what I said?
Your wish. What was it?"

"You know how it is with wishes," Tori replied,
excited about her decision. "You're not supposed to
talk about them."

Then she took a deep breath. "Look, Haruo, I need
your help."

"What kind of help?"

"All you have to do is go to my classroom and tell
Miss Chantrelle I'm still sick. Will you do that for
me?"

Tori knew this was a big request. She had never
trusted her brother with something so important.
Then there was always the possibility he'd tell Mama
and Papa. That could mean big trouble.

Haruo hesitated for only a moment before he said,
"You're going to find them, aren't you?"

"I am," Tori answered, excited and scared all jumbled together.

"Be careful. You don't want the truant officer to

find you. Hide if you see him. I don't know what he looks like, but it'd be awful if he caught you skipping school. Mama and Papa would never forgive you."

"I will."

"There's just one thing you have to promise."

"What's that?"

"That you'll tell me everything when you get back. Promise?"

"Promise."

"You'd better hurry then! Hurry!" Haruo shouted after Tori, who was already running to the streetcar stop.

Arriving at the corner of Grove and Stuart Streets breathing hard, Tori fidgeted while she waited. She'd taken this trip with Mama many times but never alone. She waited and waited. Will the streetcar ever arrive? As the minutes ticked by, Tori's enthusiasm about her plan began to fade.

That's when she saw the man. Dressed in a dark suit and hat, he walked toward her, whistling. The whistling stopped when he noticed her. Briskly, he headed her way.

The truant officer! Tori's felt dizzy. He'd arrest her or take her to Principal Bradley's office, or worse yet, he'd take her home to Mama. Tori froze.

"What are you doing here, little girl?" he asked.

Tori's mind raced—truth or fib? Truth or fib? Maybe a bit of both.

"I'm going to see some friends. They lost everything in the fire."

"Awful, isn't it? I've got lots of friends in the same boat. Terrible, just terrible." He shook his head, quiet for a moment. "But you'll never get there if you wait here," he added.

"What do you mean?"

"This streetcar line isn't working yet. Not allowed into the fire area. In fact, it may be several days before that happens. You could wait here all day but not one will come by."

He smiled, tipped his hat and continued on his way.

Tori let out her breath. He wasn't the truant officer after all. But the streetcar, oh no! What should she do? Walking to Polly's would take at least an hour. Or should she go to campus? That's not as far. They could be there—or not. It'll take all morning to find them, if she's lucky. Then she'd have to walk back, all before three o'clock when Mama would be waiting for her. Maybe she should give up, turn around, and head back to school. How silly to think she could do this! If she left now, she'd be only a few minutes late.

A loud yell distracted her. Down the street in his

battered, creaky truck rolled Old Yugoro, the fruit and produce man. Driving slowly, he announced his arrival to all the housewives in the neighborhood with his call, "Fruit and vegetables, fruit and vegetables! Come and get your fruit and vegetables!" You could hear him blocks away.

Mama always said he had the best produce in town, delivered fresh every morning from his son's farm. She often sent Tori running after Old Yugoro's truck with money for his goods. He never said much but he seemed friendly. Would he give her a ride? Even a few blocks would help. Tori was certain he'd recognize her. As the truck neared, Tori waved. He stopped in front of her.

"Hello, Little One. You are far from home."

"Yes, I guess so. I'm on an errand but the streetcars aren't running. Please, could you take me to University Avenue? I can give you two pennies. I know that Mama and Papa would be most grateful."

Behind her back, Tori crossed her fingers like Polly did when she told a small fib.

"Keep your pennies, Little One. I will take you. I have been looking for an excuse to see the fire."

Tori could hardly believe her good luck. While she bounced along in the truck's front seat, she could hear Polly's words in her head. "Quick thinking saved the day." True, Tori had told a fib, but for a good reason. Now all she had to do was find her friends. She'd start at Spruce Street, and if that didn't work out, then she'd go to campus. The truck moved slowly through traffic, its noisy motor chugging steadily. Tori was thankful to be on Yugoro's truck rather than on one with all those fish. That would have been a smelly ride. Luckily, the sweet scent of ripe fruit and fresh greens surrounded her.

The truck ride went quickly. Soon Yugoro pulled up to the same corner where Tori had watched the red glowing fire light up the night sky. The old man parked alongside the curb. He was silent. Tori knew why. A vast empty space stretched out before them. Except for the lonely chimneys standing watch, nothing was left. Not one tree, not one house, not one beautiful thing, for blocks and blocks. Some small part of Tori had hoped the fire was a bad dream. It wasn't.

Everything looked as she remembered, with one exception. Now, long lines of wood sawhorses snaked around the fire-ruined neighborhood. Soldiers with rifles stood by them. Long lines of people waited patiently for the soldiers to check a piece of paper they carried. Tori shuddered. Why did the soldiers have guns? Would they shoot her if she tried to get into the neighborhood without that special paper? How would she ever get to Spruce Street now?

Tori wanted to stay in the safety of the truck. But she had no choice. She couldn't sit next to Yugoro forever. Reluctantly, she climbed down from the truck's cab.

"Thanks for the ride," she said in her most polite voice.

Good humor gone, Yugoro grunted, tipped his cap, and sat stone-like, staring ahead.

Although no one seemed to notice Tori standing there, she felt uneasy. *Me and my dumb ideas, she thought. Why did I ever think I could actually find Jerry and Polly, give them the nickel, and get back home without Mama and Papa knowing? But Polly and Jerry are my friends. Isn't that what friends do for each other?*

Tori decided to take one last look at the barricade before starting her long walk home. Even though she didn't want to cry, tears came anyhow. About to leave, she saw a small group of children race into a nearby grocery store, the screen door banging behind them. She recognized the store immediately—Polly and Jerry's favorite place for candy. The one she always avoided.

Polly and Jerry had never asked Tori why she wouldn't go with them. She was glad about that. How could she tell them she was afraid the owner would give her that look, the one that said *you're not welcome here, little Japanese girl.* Tori never wanted that to happen, especially in front of her friends.

If only I could be invisible, she wished. She squeezed the wooden nickel in her pocket as she imagined going into the store like an unseen ghost, buying candy for her friends, and walking right past the soldiers. Just as quickly, Tori let go of the coin. Even though she didn't believe in wishes and magic, she wasn't taking any chances. But now she had an idea. Was she brave enough?

One of Polly's favorite sayings popped into her mind—"You'll never know unless you try!" Polly said this whenever she wanted to make Tori and Jerry do something weird or scary. *You'll never know unless you try! You'll never know unless you try!* Despite her fear, Tori made up her mind to buy something for Jerry and Polly, no matter if the owner gave her a funny look. Tori would do it for her friends before walking home. She had to. *You'll never know unless you try!*

The dimly lit store reminded Tori of the one in her own neighborhood—ceiling fan overhead, small narrow aisles, and the wooden counter with its shiny brass cash register sitting next to boxes of penny candies. There were brightly colored jawbreakers, Jujubees, and chewy chocolate babies the size of her pinky. The cool, dark interior even smelled the same—a mixture of pungent spices, freshly ground coffee beans, and soap powder. Tori waited for her turn behind the group of children, milk money clutched in her sweaty hand, her mouth suddenly dry. The children didn't seem to notice her at all. They were too busy with talk of the fire.

"The only thing we found this morning were a few of Tommy's metal train cars," said a redheaded, freckle-faced girl in front of Tori. "Momma says we have to go back to school tomorrow. But I only have this one dress."

"We have to move in with my grandparents," griped a tall, thin boy, wrinkling his nose. "They live in Oakland."

"One of the soldiers let me hold his gun," said another little boy.

When he smiled, Tori could see he was missing the same front teeth as Kenji's.

"I'm going to be a soldier someday," he confided earnestly to his friends.

Tori knew exactly what to buy when it was her turn—miniature root beer barrels, three for one penny. She would get six, three for Polly and three for Jerry. She knew how much they loved biting off the candy's wax top and drinking the little bit of root beer before chewing the rest of the wax barrel until all its sweetness disappeared. Only one more child to go. Would the store owner notice that Tori didn't belong here? Her knees felt weak. It was her turn.

"Now young lady, what would you like?"

"Two pennies' worth of root beer barrels, please."

"What'd you say?" asked the man, cupping his hand to his ear. "You'll have to speak up. My hearing isn't so good anymore."

"Two pennies' worth of root beer barrels, please," she repeated, a little louder.

The owner put the six candies in a tiny brown paper bag, folded the top neatly, and tossed her pennies into the cash register's coin tray. Then he looked at Tori over the rim of his glasses. Tori held her breath.

"Thank-you, little miss," he said. That was all. No funny looks, no nasty words, nothing. Just thank-you.

A shake of the paper bag reassured her. She'd done it! Now if she could figure out how to deliver the candy to Polly and Jerry. By now the children had made their way to the barricades. Tori watched. The soldiers barely glanced at them. Would it be the same for her? *You'll never know unless you try!*

It all turned out perfectly! Seconds later she was standing on the other side of the roadblock. She'd done it! Wouldn't Polly and Jerry be surprised!

The pack of children raced on ahead. Tori walked slowly, stunned by the ruins that surrounded her. Families sifted through the rubbish that had once been their homes, using sticks to poke at the ashes, bricks, and twisted metal. That's what I can do, Tori realized. I can help Polly and Jerry look through the ashes for some little thing worth keeping.

Soon she came to Spruce Street, a few blocks from where Polly's house used to be. Surprisingly, a few homes still stood. The farther she walked the more homes she saw, miraculously untouched. Hadn't Agnes said there were burning houses everywhere? None of this made sense. Finally at Cedar and Spruce, Tori braced herself for the worst.

In place of houses on either side of the street, debris-filled lots were all that remained. But what was that ahead? It looked just like Polly's house, standing all alone. She rubbed her eyes. No, it *was* Polly's house! She was sure of it. The Wetherby house was really gone, but sitting next door was the Griffin home, the Berman double-decker behind it, and the biggest miracle of all, the bamboo garden with its tall green stalks still swaying in the breeze.

She ran past the Wetherby lot. Before her Monday night adventure with Agnes, Tori hadn't cared one bit what happened to the nasty girl. Now she wondered about them. Where were they living? At that instant a terrible idea burst into Tori's head. Polly's wish came true. Poof, the Wetherby house had disappeared. That was only part of Polly's wish. Sadly,

Tori knew the other part would never come true. The Takahashi family would never be allowed to buy a house here.

Tori ran the rest of the way, past the front porch, and along the driveway to the back door. She pounded on it and waited. From deep within the house, Tori heard footsteps. The knob turned. Slowly, the door opened. Standing there, with a furry, blue-eyed, lop-eared bunny clutched to her chest—was Polly Griffin.

"Tori!" Polly's excited shout frightened Fudge right out of her arms.

Tori scooped up the bunny, gave her a gentle hug, and handed her back to Polly. Next she pulled the wooden nickel from her pocket. "Here Polly. It's yours now."

Wordlessly Polly took the nickel, carefully putting it in a dress pocket. That was the easy part, thought Tori. Breathlessly, she went on. "My wish came true, you know."

"Oh, my gosh," Polly whispered hoarsely. "What was it? Tell me everything!"

"It had to do with friends." Now Tori felt shy and awkward. She forced herself go on. "But I have one . . . a really good one . . . a best friend." Tori stepped forward and hugged Polly and her bunny as she said, "And that best friend is you!"

Polly smiled. "You've always been my best friend, Tori, and you always will be." After hugging Tori back, she added, "I've been thinking that Agnes may have been right about one thing." Polly switched Fudge to her other shoulder. "Maybe we are odd-balls—best friends who don't even go to the same school. But, come on! We've got even more important things to talk about."

Tori ran with Polly, right into the center of the bamboo grove's enchanted circle. After Polly settled Fudge in her lap, she began.

"There's something I've wanted to tell you for a really long time," Polly said using her most dramatic voice. "But then the fire and everything got in the way. There was no . . . "

A shout from Mrs. Griffin interrupted Polly. "Polls, where are you! Get in here this minute!"

Ignoring her mother's call, Polly grabbed Tori's hands. "Nothing's going to keep me from telling you. You just have to hear this. Tori, I've discovered the most wonderful thing about those laws. I know you don't want to think about them. Neither do I. But listen. I know you're going to be happy!"

What Polly told her about the loophole and how Tori could help her parents had to be the most magical moment of this magical day.

Chapter Twenty-Two

❧ Tori ❧

Just a few more weeds and Tori would be finished cleaning up around the young bamboo shoots, now as tall as the fence. Papa would be pleased, and she still had plenty of time to get dressed in her good clothes. A bright sun and cool breeze promised that the first Annual Family Cookie Exchange would be a success.

Was it only last week when she and Polly got the idea for the Cookie Exchange? Tori had been sitting on the Griffins' front porch swing with Polly. Fudge was asleep between them. They were munching Mrs. Hastings' cinnamony snickerdoodles.

"I wish my mother knew how to make these," Tori had said with a sigh. "They're the best."

"Well, what does your mother make that you really,

really like?" Polly asked, cookie crumbs dotting the front of her blouse.

"*Mochi.*"

"Mochi—what's that?"

Tori had tried to describe the soft, sweet, chewy treat. Polly didn't seem to understand any of it. Frustrated, she said, "Sounds like the only way I'm going to know what you're talking about is to taste it myself."

"That won't be so easy," Tori laughed. "Making mochi is hard. It's special, too. We have to wait for Oshogatsu to get some."

"What's Oshogatsu?"

"The Japanese New Year."

"Does it *have* to be New Year's to eat it?"

"No."

Polly nibbled her cookie around the edges, making it into a smaller and smaller circle until it disappeared. Then, dusting off the crumbs she jumped from the swing and stood in front of Tori.

"I do believe I've just thought up my best idea ever!"

"Uh, oh!"

"No, just listen." Polly settled herself on the porch railing before going on. "Now, you know I'd really like to try this mochi, right?"

"Right."

"And you really like snickerdoodles but your mother never bakes them, right?"

"Right."

"Well, do you think your mother would, if she had the recipe?"

"Maybe."

"OK, last question. Who makes the best cookies in the world?"

That was an easy one. Tori smiled as she remembered how together they had shouted, "Mrs. Berman!"

The rest of that afternoon had been spent in the Griffins' bamboo grove planning the first Annual Family Cookie Exchange. When they asked Mrs. Griffin to help, she didn't need any convincing, the same for Mrs. Berman, Aunt Charlotte, and the biggest surprise of all—Mama!

Because she had the best handwriting, Tori put the names and addresses on the envelopes. She added a small Japanese design on each one. Now the invitations looked really special. Polly did the insides. Even though she used all the colors in the rainbow for the words, Tori liked how it came out. Everyone said they would be delighted to attend.

Yesterday, Tori went over to help Polly fix up the garden. Jerry gave them a hand. They moved the picnic table under the oak tree and decorated the tree with the paper chains Tori showed them how to make. After they were up, the garden became magically transformed. Tori couldn't wait for the cookie exchange, but the sleepover afterwards would be even more exciting.

Finally the big day arrived. Just one more weed and Tori would be done. Straightening up to admire her work, she was surprised by Papa.

"You're up early, Toriko!" he said stretching, hands reaching for the sky.

"Yes, Papa, I wanted to surprise you. Don't you think our bamboo is growing well?"

"Very well, my daughter, especially under your watchful eye. Soon it will be tall and strong enough for me to show you some tricks I learned as a boy."

"What kinds of tricks, Papa?"

"We can use some of its sturdy stalk to build a fountain for water. One piece is all we need. The hollow core will make a fine pipe for dripping water into our little pond. For Mama, we shall make a wind chime. It will remind her of home."

"Which home are you talking about, Papa?"

"The home where I spent my boyhood, Toriko — Japan. But this is my home, too. I have two homes, I guess," he said, a slight smile brightening his usually somber face.

"I think you'll like the Griffins' home, Papa. There're going to be lots of people coming. But they're all very nice. Millie and Donald can't come because there's a football game. But, of course you'll finally meet Polly and Jerry."

"I know I'll like your friends. Now, I'd better do a little work out here before Mama makes me put on my good clothes and my best manners." He laughed at his own joke.

On the streetcar ride to Spruce Street, Tori couldn't help feeling proud. The Takahashi family always looked nice when they dressed up for church, but today they looked even more special. Mama wore a new dress, soft gray with navy trim. The top part rested low on her hips, with a pleated skirt to just below her knees. She had asked Tori about which hat to wear. After considering two choices, Tori selected the navy one. It was a lot like Mrs. Griffin's favorite style — snug and sitting low across her forehead. Mama's had pink flowers around the brim.

Even though Mama didn't say anything about how Tori looked in her new blue dress, she could tell Mama liked it. "I should make more dresses for you in this color, Toriko," she said, buttoning up the back.

Papa looked handsome in his dark slacks and white shirt, but the hat nearly gave Tori the giggles. He had bought it especially for today after Mama told him he couldn't wear his well-used cloth cap. With this new, wide-brimmed felt hat, Papa looked just like the men Tori had seen at the streetcar stop, carrying the newspapers they would read on the ferry to San Francisco. Mama had insisted the boys wear sweaters that matched their knickers — Haruo in blue and Kenji in brown. Even little Yoshi wore something special, a navy-and-white sailor suit.

Mama wouldn't let anyone else carry the shiny red lacquer tray filled with its precious mochi. Just thinking about biting through the soft chewy outside on the way to the sweet bean-paste center made Tori's mouth water. Mama and Papa had worked many hours to make these rice-flour goodies. While Papa pounded the rice, Mama had stirred, and then there was all the work shaping and steaming the candies.

The streetcar was so packed that everyone had to stand except for Mama. She sat, holding on her lap the covered tray of sweets wrapped in colorful cloth she had tied into a fancy bow.

As Tori hopped off the streetcar's last step, she was eager to tell her family about all the changes of the last two months.

"Papa, I'm glad you get to see the neighborhood now. For weeks now trucks have been taking away all the burned-up junk and ashes."

"Did they find any bodies?" Kenji asked.

Haruo took off his cap and gave Kenji a playful swat.

"Actually, they did!" she replied, trying hard to look concerned.

"Tori, are you sure?" Papa asked. "I didn't think there were any deaths."

Tori looked solemn. "Yes, Papa, I'm sure. They found a skeleton somewhere nearby." Then, after a Polly Griffin dramatic pause, she smiled broadly and added, "Later they found out the skeleton belonged to a biology professor. He used it in his classes. It turned out that this body must have been dead long before the fire!"

Everyone laughed at her story.

"Lots of building going on," Haruo observed, as they walked by three houses with their wood framing already in place.

"I'll say," Tori agreed. "We've been watching the workmen pour concrete for new foundations. We even got to scratch our names in some of the wet cement."

It had been Polly's idea. Tori wasn't sure they should. But then Polly found the perfect place, a freshly poured foundation nearby where no one would ever notice. Waiting in the bamboo garden for the workmen to leave, they decided what to write.

"Definitely our names," Jerry said.

"Definitely," Polly agreed.

"Don't forget the date and how old we are," Tori said.

She liked the idea that some day in the future someone might find their names and exclaim over the date. "Oh," they'd say, "look at how long ago these children wrote their names. I wonder what they're doing today."

"What about a drawing?" Jerry asked. "You know, something like those hobo drawings Smilin' Sam showed us."

"But let's make a drawing that tells about us, maybe something important to us," Tori added.

Jerry had sharpened a twig with his pocket knife, which worked great in the wet cement. Polly went first. She drew a book after her name. "I just love books," she said. "Maybe someday I'll write my own. Now wouldn't that be the bee's knees!"

Tori watched Jerry draw a baseball.

"But, Jerry, you don't even play baseball!" Tori protested.

"I know. But I want to learn. I've got a new glove."

Then it was Tori's turn. Slowly she printed her name T-O-R-I. Then she drew some Japanese characters. For once she was pleased she'd gone to Japanese school all those afternoons after regular school.

"Oh, pretty. What did you draw?" Polly asked.

"My name in Japanese," said Tori. "See, it says *tori*. That means bird."

"That's so neat! Your name means something!" Polly exclaimed.

Tori liked the idea of leaving her Japanese name in this other part of Berkeley, a place she loved.

Chapter Twenty-Three

❦ Tori ❦

Tori had gotten used to the sound of hammering and sawing on her visits to Spruce Street. Today, the neighborhood was surprisingly quiet.

So far the Wetherby house was only a wood frame, but even so it already looked grand. The hedge that had separated the Wetherbys' house from the Griffins' had been destroyed by the fire, leaving a line of burnt twigs. No more hiding place. Last Saturday Tori watched Agnes and her parents walk around their unfinished first floor. Agnes's little brother and sister ran up and down the half-done staircase.

Tori and Agnes had waved hello to each other. Jerry and Polly had pretended not to see. Tori had understood. They hadn't seen Agnes that night of the fire, the tears, and the hurt. They hadn't heard her actually say *thank-you*.

The Bamboo Garden

As the Takahashi family approached the Griffins' front porch, Tori realized something new was about to happen. Mama would be walking through the front door. She would be a guest. New worries sprinkled down on Tori. Would her brothers behave? Would Mama and Papa's English be good enough? Would they enjoy themselves?

Tori had only seconds to worry. Jerry and Polly were waiting for them. They looked surprisingly grown-up in their good clothes. Suddenly awkward, Tori didn't know what to do next. But Polly jumped right in.

"These must be your little brothers, Tori. Aren't they adorable! I'll bet you're Kenji and you have to be Haruo. Oh, I know all about you two! I'm so glad you could come. Gosh, Yoshi, aren't you just the cutest little thing!"

Relieved, Tori watched Haruo and Kenji remember to take off their caps. To Tori's surprise, Yoshi held his arms out to Polly. She picked him up, planted a big kiss on his chubby pink cheek, and then said to everyone, "Won't you please come in?"

Tori had never seen her friend in the role of the charming hostess. Thank goodness, Mrs. Griffin took over in the front hall. Professor Griffin joined her.

"Mr. and Mrs. Takahashi! Welcome," Professor Griffin said. Then, vigorously shaking Papa's hand, he added, "So glad you are here. Come on outside and let me introduce you around. You arrived in the nick of time. We sure could use your advice."

Tori glanced at Papa. She'd never seen him with non-Japanese people. After neatly placing his hat on the hallway rack, Papa walked with Professor Griffin through the house and to the garden as if he'd been there a million times. She watched him shake hands with Professor Cole and Polly's Uncle Horace.

Professor Griffin's booming voice made it easy for Tori to overhear. "You see, Mr. Takahashi, Horace here is very concerned about his property. We were just discussing what he should do to keep from losing too much topsoil this winter during the rains. He's not going to be able to rebuild until spring."

The women had gathered around Mama, exclaiming over her tray.

"What a marvelous idea," Mrs. Griffin exclaimed.

"Absolutely beautiful," agreed Aunt Charlotte.

"I can't wait to try these, Mrs. Takahashi," Mrs. Berman joined in. "Tori told me you were going to make something special. She assured me that mochi will be a new and wonderful experience."

Platters of cookies filled the table, pitchers of lemonade at either end. Mrs. Griffin had let the girls take out her fancy dessert plates. Tori couldn't have been more proud. Everyone seemed to be having a good time, but would they like the mochi? She watched as Mrs. Griffin took her first small nibble. Her next bites were bigger. Everyone wanted to know how pounding rice could make such a smooth, sweet morsel. Mama and Papa tried to explain, but from the puzzled expressions around the table, Tori knew they didn't understand.

Tori tasted every cookie on the table. The best part of their cookie exchange was that Mrs. Griffin, Mrs. Berman, and Aunt Charlotte had written out their recipes on little cards for Mama. Everyone brought so many cookies, Tori knew the last part of their plan was going to work. There'd be plenty of extras to bring home.

When all the guests had their fill of cookies, Tori and Polly traded glances. The moment had arrived. It had been Polly's idea, and Tori loved it even if she doubted she'd be able to carry it off.

Polly stood up and with her spoon gently tapped on her lemonade glass. Polly had prepared Tori for this—her father's way of making an announcement at the table. Everyone quieted down after the first few taps and looked at Polly.

"Ahem," Polly said, clearing her throat. "Tori and I have something to share with everyone."

The two girls had rehearsed for days. Tori's turn came next. Her mouth felt as dry as a bread crust. Thank goodness there were lots of smiles.

"I'm sure everyone here knows about Mrs. Berman and Professor Cole getting married. We think it's wonderful for them, and, of course, for Jerry."

Tori looked over at Jerry to see what effect her words had on her friend. He turned beet red. Next came Polly.

"We have a little gift for them. It's sure to bring good things their way, or at least we hope so."

With that, Polly took a tiny white box from her dress pocket. She handed it to Mrs. Berman.

"We hope you will both be very happy," Tori said.

"And Jerry, too," Polly added.

Everybody applauded and then watched expectantly as Mrs. Berman untied the red ribbon. She gave the box to Professor Cole to open.

Carefully removing the lid, he said, "I can't imagine what treasure this little box could hold, but I'm sure . . . " He never finished the sentence. "Oh, my gosh. Now, would you look at that!" Between his thumb and forefinger, he held up a tiny wood-carved nickel.

The coin led to lots of chatter about Smilin' Sam, Professor Cole's interest in hoboes, and what these little charms could mean. Tori told everyone how she found Smilin' Sam under the berry bush, her shyness gone. They laughed hard at the part about Polly thinking she'd seen an elf.

"That's my little girl," Professor Griffin said beaming. "What an imagination!"

He laughed so hard, Tori thought he might never stop. She'd never seen him this jolly. Perhaps his cheerfulness had something to do with his book — the really, really important book — finally getting published.

Tori thought Polly and Jerry did a good job telling their different ideas about Smilin' Sam.

"Jerry never did warm up to him, did you, Jer?" Polly asked.

"No, but I have a good reason." A huge grin spread over his face. "Never trust anyone who uses a rope to hold up his pants!"

The afternoon ended in the living room. First, Mrs. Griffin played a piano duet with Aunt Charlotte. Then, Professor Griffin stood in front of the fireplace and read a long poem. His deep, melodious voice had the three Takahashi brothers sound asleep long before he came to the last line. Even Tori struggled to stay awake.

Later, after all the guests had left, Tori helped

Polly bring piles of blankets and pillows into the living room. They made their beds on the floor in front of the dying fire.

"Oh, Tori, wasn't this the best ever?"

"The best," Tori agreed. "Mama and Papa seemed to have a good time. I wasn't sure they would. I mean, everything was kind of upside-down."

Polly was silent. This pleased Tori. It had taken a long time for her to want to share these kinds of thoughts with Polly. Before, she couldn't be sure Polly would understand. Today Mama wasn't the maid. Papa wasn't the man in the soil-stained work clothes. They were guests. They had enjoyed themselves.

"I just didn't know what to expect," Tori finally confessed.

"I know what you mean. It must have felt funny, for all of you. But Mother and Father think the world of you and your mom. They couldn't wait to meet the rest of your family." After a brief pause, Polly added, "I'm still surprised that Mother knew a lot more about Agnes and the Wetherbys than we had thought. I told you about that, didn't I?"

Even though Polly had, Tori let her tell it again.

"Mother and Father thought I was too young to hear about things like prejudice. But I don't think you're ever too young to learn this kind of stuff. Father has a name for people who hate everyone who's different from themselves. 'Small-minded' is what he calls them."

"It's funny, Polly. Even though I still don't like the Wetherbys, Agnes doesn't seem so awful anymore. Sometimes, I even feel a little sorry for her."

The fire's flickering glow created beautiful patterns on the ceiling. Logs crackled and snapped. Funny how fire can be so pretty and so awful, Tori thought.

Ever since the big fire, Tori had noticed a change in their friendship. Lately, Polly wanted to talk about things that really mattered to Tori, such as why there were people like the Wetherbys. Polly also seemed more interested in what went on in the Takahashi home. This made Tori feel brave enough to invite Polly for their New Year's celebration at church.

"Does everyone wear kimonos at Oshogatsu?" Polly asked.

"Sure, even the men."

"I'd love to wear one. Could I?"

"Yep, I have one just your size. But, you'll have to dance, too, you know."

"Dance?" asked Polly. "But I don't know how."

"I'll teach you. It's really simple. All you have to do is follow me."

"Can I help with the mochi, too? I'd love to pound that rice."

"You'll get a turn. Everybody does."

Polly slipped out from under her blankets and sat on her knees facing Tori. Tori rolled over so she could see her friend. Flame shadows danced across Polly's face.

"Didn't Jerry look happy tonight? He just couldn't stop smiling. That was his wish, you know, something for his mom. He says Professor Cole is going to build a house for them up in the hills. He says it should be ready by springtime. I love weddings, don't you, Tori?

"I've never been to a wedding," Tori said, "but if Mrs. Berman is doing any of the baking, then I'm sure I'll love it."

"Jerry says that Professor Cole asked him to be his Best Man."

"You know, Polly, I think this wedding has Jerry more excited than when his wireless finally worked!"

"I'm sure going to miss having him nearby. But he won't be too far away, and we can go visit him all the time. It's kind of like you and me. Why, here we are, best friends, and we don't live next door, do we?"

It turned out that even though Polly had been right about the loophole, Mama and Papa explained to Tori that they still couldn't buy a house on the other side of town. "It just isn't allowed," was all they said. But thank goodness Polly finally gave up on the idea of the Takahashis living next door to the Griffins.

Tori knew she and Polly would always be best friends. She also knew there would be other friends in their lives, like that new girl Polly invited over last week. The costume the girl dreamed up for Polly's latest theatrical production was so hilarious the three giggled until their stomachs hurt.

Polly continued to chatter about the afternoon, about how nice Tori's parents were, about how cute baby Yoshi was, about how Kenji and Haruo almost looked like twins except for their height, and on and on. The popping of the fire's embers and Polly's voice, the cozy warmth of the blankets wrapped tightly around her lulled Tori into a drowsy mood. Polly's voice started to fade. That is, until Polly shook her shoulder.

"Hey, Tori, what do you think? Isn't that a grand idea?"

"What, Polly?" Tori mumbled sleepily.

"You know, that someday we'll go to the university together. We can be roommates. Of course, I'd really prefer the top bunk. But you can have it if you want. I think I'll study English, and maybe you'll study something like art or French. After we graduate, we can travel to Europe together, and then . . . "

Tori smiled, snuggled farther under her covers, and decided that whether or not Polly's dreams ever come true, whatever happens, she was ready.

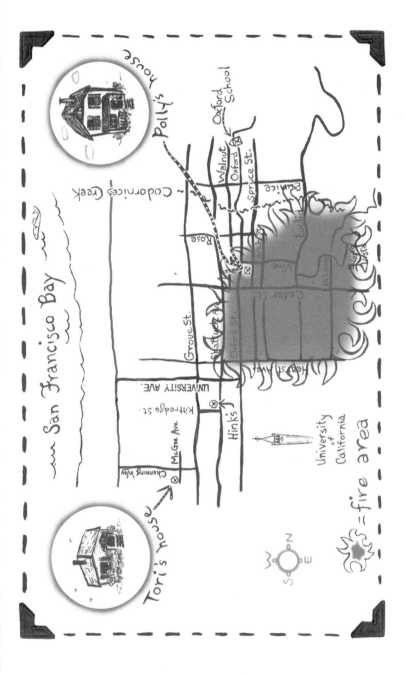

Notes from the Author

Are you curious about which part of this book is true and which is made up? The answer is simple. Everything in *The Bamboo Garden* is absolutely true, with one gigantic exception: Polly Griffin and Tori Takahashi. I invented them along with their families, friends, neighbors, and pet bunny. I did not invent the details of the neighborhoods where the girls lived, the horrendous fire that swept over Berkeley, or the laws specifically targeting Japanese Americans.

The Griffin and Takahashi Houses and Neighborhoods

I picked two different Berkeley neighborhoods for the girls. Tori's house is in the part of Berkeley where most of the Japanese American families lived in 1923, filled with small, modest homes. Polly lives in a spacious shake-shingled home on the other side of town close to the university where her father teaches. From a special map that shows which houses survived the fire and which were burned down, I selected Polly's

Spruce Street house for one reason — it was one of the few that miraculously survived the fire while others nearby were destroyed.

The Famous Fire of September 23, 1923

Everything about the fire is precisely how it happened. Old photographs and newspaper accounts were a treasure trove for learning about the days leading up to the fire and the days that followed. Luckily, several Berkeley residents wrote about their experiences during the most horrifying hours. Many of the details in their eyewitness accounts were woven into this story. For example, the weather had been beastly hot all summer, made worse by a lack of rain and bay fog to cool things down — perfect conditions to ignite the town. Do you remember how long it took for Mrs. Griffin to decide what to do? Well, that was true for many people. They could not believe a fire was about to sweep over them. Yes, cars did come rushing down the hill crammed full of household animals and frightened pets, and at least one with a cow tethered to its bumper. The Berkeley hills fire was one of several fires burning simultaneously. Other uncontrolled fires burned above the university campus and in nearby Oakland. If it were not for a sudden change in wind at four o'clock in the afternoon, everything could have been far worse.

The Bamboo Garden

The Anti-Japanese Laws

The 1920s were a period in U.S. history of widespread prejudice toward all minorities. The California Land Law of 1913 prevented Japanese immigrants from buying farmland. Other states passed similar laws, and cities established local ordinances and zoning laws that prohibited Asians and African Americans from buying or renting in certain neighborhoods.

Although these were shameful times, Polly and Tori saw that not everyone supported discrimination and that they did not need to live next door to each other to have a strong and lasting friendship. More importantly, they learned what their friendship needed most—honesty and courage.

One Last Thing

Picking names for characters in a book is great fun and very important. Sometimes authors pick names because of their secret meaning. I thought you might like to know how Tori got her last name—Takahashi. *Hashi* (the last part of her name) has two meanings in Japanese. *Hashi* can mean chopsticks, but it can also mean bridge. I like to think that Tori's last name refers to the way her friendship with Polly represents building a bridge between their different cultures.

Acknowledgments

Early in the creation of this book Mary Tolman Kent and Deborah Tolman Whitney shared stories with me about growing up in the Tolman household during the 1920s in Berkeley. A passing remark about their Japanese maid inspired my creation of the unlikely friendship between Tori and Polly.

Thanks to all who played a role in *The Bamboo Garden:*

To Edie Meidev for her wise and skillful mentorship when *The Bamboo Garden* was little more than a vague idea and to Deborah Brody who knows her way to a story's heart.

To the Berkeley Historical Society and its treasure trove of memorabilia — a veritable gold mine of material for historical fiction writers. A special thanks to Steven Finacom, John Aronovici and the late Ken Cardwell whose knowledge and passion for Berkeley history was of invaluable assistance.

To the Berkeley Writer's Workshop for their support and interest, especially Mary Alyce Pearson. A special thanks to The Novel Group whose feedback enriched every word: Betsy Behrens, Diane DePisa, Marge Judge, Mary Kent, Sharon Kaye, Joan Mastronarde, and Mary Parks.

To my willing and insightful reviewers: Michiko Uchida, Susan Nuñes Fadley, Kimberlee Austin, Phyllis Smith, Adela Karliner, and Margery Hellmann.

To all the children who entered the world of Polly and Tori with enthusiasm and curiosity, and especially: Hannah Curtiss, Alyssa Keimach and Alyssa's Mother/Daughter Book Group, Emily Sara Austin and Mia Austin Graham.

To Felicia Hoshino for the beautiful and sensitive artwork that graces the cover of this book and to Suzanne Klein for her charming visual representation of Berkeley in 1923.

To those editors who taught me the value of the simple but powerful comma: Sue Mann and David Brownell, and to Jennifer Omner, a book designer with style.

To my husband, Mike, for his nearly endless patience and loving support.

About the Author

S usan Austin, Ph.D., author and educator, lives in Berkeley, California, the setting for *The Bamboo Garden*. Writing books about long ago gives her a creative outlet for exploring themes that matter—friendship, prejudice, and courage.

She grew up in Los Angeles, California where a wise and passionate poet, Ruth Le Prade, helped her explore these important ideas. Miss Le Prade lived a few doors away and would invite Susan and other neighborhood children to her home to listen to poetry about beauty and compassion. Every visit ended with a romp in her magical garden of exotic trees and flowering bushes planted by poets visiting from distant lands. In the far corner of her garden grew a towering grove of bamboo—Susan's favorite place to play and dream.

Susan Austin

Susan's best writing ideas show up as she prunes her prickly rose bushes or combs Santa Cruz beaches for delicate pieces of colored sea glass. Currently, she is putting the finishing touches on her latest book: *Just the Ticket: A Summer Adventure-by-the-Sea.*